THE TIMEKEEPER'S APPRENTICE

ISBN 978-0-473-50928-6

THE TIMEKEEPER'S APPRENTICE

CORNELIUS JONES

To all of you who made Aethasia a reality.
From code, to pixels, downloads and installs.
Dreams, donations, investment and prayer.
And to Jesus who made this entire grand adventure possible.
Not a day goes by that we are not grateful.

Tim Cleary and the Aetherlight team.

CHAPTER ONE

IT WAS LATE afternoon when the horse and cart pulled up on the forest road outside the ornate gates of Everbright Manor. Behind the wagon, to the east, the sun was beginning to sink, over beyond No Man's Landing where their long journey had begun. There was a sudden chill in the air as a breeze scattered autumn leaves across the road, and Magda Everbright pulled her scarf more closely to her neck and leaned in against her young husband as she gazed through the gates to the house.

"Would you look at that?" she said, her mouth agape in wonder.

"You'll catch flies with your mouth open so wide," said Jude. "Anyway, it's nothing special."

"Nothing special? It's, it's..."

"It's a house, nothing more, nothing less."

"You're incorrigible, Mr. Everbright," said Magda, teasing.

"Nothing I ain't owned up to," Jude said. "Anyway, close that mouth of yours and let's be getting inside. He'll be here soon."

Jude Everbright climbed from the cart and came around to help his wife. She was stiff from the long journey west and her legs were sore, so she had to dismount backwards with her backside in the air as if she was climbing out of a window.

"These blasted skirts," Magda moaned, her feet caught up in the frills of her petticoat. "I'll break my neck on these things one day, I will."

"Come on dear, stop your fussing and give me your hand. Or would you like me to carry you?"

"Hmph, who do you think you are, Mr Everbright, so strong all of a sudden? You did a grand job carrying me over the threshold on our wedding day, but I've put on some pounds in the twelve months since."

"You look lovelier than ever," said Jude, with not a hint of sarcasm.

"Oh…you!"

Magda managed to get both feet on the ground and steadied herself by holding onto the side of the cart, right above where the Everbright & Sons sign had been nailed to sideboards.

"I'll never get used to this name." She traced the carved letters with her finger. She was puffing like she'd run a mile.

"A bit winded there, my love?"

"It's heavy work lugging all this fancy clobber around," she said. "You should try it sometime, Mr. Everbright, with your fancy waistcoat and sharp suits."

Jude pulled himself straighter. "Mrs. Everbright, a gentleman of Evercity needs to look his best. I'm not just anyone, you know. I may even be someone important someday. Now hush for a moment, my love, while I take a closer look at the grounds."

Strapped to his bowler hat and secured by a leather toggle was a pair of mechanical goggles, which he pulled down and placed over his eyes. Magda giggled when she saw, because his eyes were suddenly the size of small eggs behind the thick, glass lenses. And no wonder—they were specially made to enhance the wearer's vision, and he scoured the grounds of the manor through the bars of the gate without having to move an inch.

"Do you see anything?" Magda put a hand on his back and peered over his shoulder through the gates.

"Not a thing," Jude answered. "It's just as he said."

"Are the gardens as beautiful as we were told?"

"Perhaps more so. Though, as you know, I'm not one for gardens."

"What sort of gardens can you see?"

"Oh, the usual. Your rose gardens, your flower beds, your manicured hedges, your great lawns, your copse of trees, your tropical greenhouse."

"They say he planted every garden himself in just six days."

"Codswallop!" said Jude. "Even the Great Engineer couldn't have done all this in a week."

"So no sign of anyone lurking about?"

"No sign at all."

"We'd better be getting in there, then."

Magda opened the crocheted purse she carried and pulled out a large key, which she offered to her husband. Jude grabbed for it but missed the key entirely, because he still wore his goggles and thought the key was much closer than it was.

"Take off the goggles, silly!" Magda laughed.

Jude did so, then took the key from his wife's hand and strode cautiously to the gate. The key fit the big lock perfectly, and when Jude gave it a turn it clicked and the gates began to swing open.

"Even the gates are wonderfully made," Magda observed.

"All right, all right," said Jude, grumpily, because he'd heard quite enough about his cousin's family and the splendour of their house and gardens. "Let's be getting in there. Don't forget the parcel."

The parcel Jude referred to was a small box that had shared the seat beside Magda all the way from Evercity, Aethasia's capital. It would have fit quite easily among their crates in the back of the cart, but Jude was adamant that it ride up front, where he could keep an eye on it.

"You can never be too sure," he'd said, packing it snugly between his wife's leg and the side of the cart.

He didn't need to be so worried, Magda thought. This was Aethasia after all, where people weren't interested in taking things that belonged to others, because there was so much to go around. The fields were lush and well-watered by the Great Engineer's pump houses, and the abundant harvests continued year after year. The rivers were replete with all manner of fish. The orchards provided fruit and olives and figs all year round and traders from around the whole world came to Aethasia with produce and art and music and crafts, so there was never a shortage of anything.

The truth was, most people were too occupied making up songs and stories to bother about pilfering from others. If anything, Aethasians were more intent on borrowing a line of verse from someone's song than they were on taking a nondescript box from somebody else's cart. But no, Jude wouldn't be convinced. The parcel had to stay upfront where he could guard it closely.

"I don't know what's got into you," Magda had said. "Who made you so nervy?"

"Never you mind," he answered, which was the answer she disliked the most because it wasn't really an answer at all.

"What's in the box, anyway?"

"I haven't the faintest idea," Jude admitted. "And I don't want to know. All he said was, make sure it's delivered. And that's what I'm doing."

The box wasn't very heavy, whatever was inside. Still, Magda handed the box to Jude, not wishing to damage it even before they'd reached the house. They walked together down the long mews towards the manor. On either side were lush lawns, perfectly manicured, almost as perfectly as the trees and hedges that lined the boundary wall of the grounds. It was a clear evening, which explained the chill, and beyond the house and the woods they could see the lower steppes of the Old Mount and the mighty Aetherswell caverns at its base.

"Look over yonder!" Jude pointed. "The crystal caves."

Magda stared. "Are you certain?"

"Of course I'm certain. Look at the colour."

Even in the fading light there was no mistaking the deep purple of the aether crystal, bursting out from the foot of the mountain like thousands of glass-blown flowers in bloom.

"It looks so lovely," Magda said, pausing for a moment. "I've heard people speak of the crystal caves but I never thought I would see them with my own eyes."

"Yes, the Aetherswell is very lovely. Now come on, my love. I don't want to be here when he returns."

The Everbright Manor was as special as the grounds that surrounded it. The closer they came, the more majestic it looked, with tall, arched windows, high gables, and turrets. Its fancy masonry comprised large blocks of stone, and it was obvious to anyone that only the finest artisans had been involved in its construction.

Magda caught her breath as she stared, and she could tell Jude was doing his very best not to be impressed at all. Nothing about the house was opulent or grandiose. It wasn't the sort of building intended to intimidate visitors, or to show off, not like some of the buildings that had sprouted in Evercity in recent years. It was just a home designed and engineered and built by artisans who loved their craft. This was no surprise, considering the master of the house was the same person who had made Aethasia such a beacon for the artisans of the world.

"What's eating you, Mr. Everbright?" Magda asked, noticing the intent frown on his face as they climbed the steps to the front door.

"Nothing," he grumbled.

"Why the grumps then?"

"This could have been my home," he muttered, but not so quietly that Magda couldn't hear it or catch its meaning.

"Now, now, Mr. Everbright," she said, slipping her arm around his waist, "envy is of no more use than a bent sprocket, as they say."

"Yes, quite," Jude said, his face flushing. They hadn't been married so long that he couldn't still be embarrassed in front of his wife. "Let's get inside while the coast is clear."

But as Jude raised his hand to the grand door knocker just to make sure, there was a great sound of steam being released from a hidden mechanism behind the walls of the manor. Jude and Magda listened as big cogs engaged little cogs, and suddenly the doors began to slide open. When the steam cleared, a tall, dark-haired boy of around ten years old stood in the doorway, ready to welcome them.

"Hello there," he said, smiling, hands clasped behind his back. "Who might you be?"

"We? Ah—well," Jude stammered, clearing his throat and blinking his eyes, "well, that depends a lot upon who *you* are."

"Me?" said the boy. "I'm Joshua. Joshua Everbright."

"Well then," said Jude. "It turns out that we are your cousins... second cousins, I believe. Is the master, erm, home?"

"I'm afraid not. He's in Evercity. There's a very important council this evening."

"Right then," Jude said. "Of course he is. Well, it seems we've come on this rather long journey for no reason. No reason at all."

"I wouldn't say that," said young Joshua, pointing at the parcel in Jude's arms. "It seems you have a box."

"Yes, yes we do," Jude said, readjusting his grip on the box.

"What's in it?" Joshua asked.

"I wouldn't know, actually," Jude said, turning to his wife as he always did, she had learned, when he didn't have a quick response. "Would you know, Magda?"

"Would I know what, Mr. Everbright?"

"What's in this box!"

"We've ascertained already that I don't, Mr. Everbright," she reminded him.

"It has my name written on the side," Joshua said.

"You are an observant little boy," Magda said, stepping forward since her husband didn't seem to know what to say. "Why don't we step inside and you can take a look?"

The great, heavy doors drew to a close behind them as they stood in the grand hall at the foot of the steps that climbed up towards the upper floor. Inside, the manor was just as refined as it was outside, with large works of art on the walls and pieces of ornate engineering standing against the sides of the hall where other grand houses might have statues and ornaments.

Everywhere, the master's unparalleled engineering talent was on display, and nowhere greater than the giant mechanical chandelier hanging from the ceiling, with arms of bronze and brass candle holders that spun as the arms rose and fell like an octopus. The window shutters were mechanical also, with great levers that triggered fancy pulley devices that lowered heavy bronze plates over the windows.

"This house is stupendous," Magda said. "The Great Engineer is so clever."

"Thank you," said Joshua. "I'm constantly telling him that myself."

"I'll bet you are," said Jude. "But listen, I'm afraid we can't stay, so how about we leave this here and be on our way?"

But Joshua would not hear of it. It wouldn't be hospitable, he explained, and if there was one thing he'd learnt from the master of the house, it was that he should be hospitable with anyone and everyone, no matter their standing in society, and no matter their background. Joshua rang for the butler and ordered tea and cakes, then led Jude and Magda into the front sitting room. As they settled down to their tea, Joshua picked up the box which Jude had placed on the table, and began to open it.

Jude rushed to replace his teacup on its saucer and jumped up from his chair. "Really, there's no need!" he insisted. "We really must be on our way. You can open it when we're gone."

But the parcel was open already, and Joshua was reading the card that had been placed inside.

BETTER TO RULE A BROKEN AETHASIA
THAN TO SERVE IN PARADISE

Joshua sat frowning, appearing to ponder the message.

"Is this from...?" he began.

"I don't know who it's from," Jude cut him off. "It was given to us in haste, by an officer of the court in Evercity. He said it was vitally important that we brought it here in time."

"In time for what?"

Jude hesitated, glancing away and shuffling his feet. "Erm, I'm not sure."

But Joshua wasn't paying much attention to Jude. He had taken his gift from the box. It was a mechanical bird, about the size and shape of a song thrush, like those that made their nests in the low hedges around the grounds. In place of feathers its wings and body were covered in small plates of copper, each one as thin as a piece of parchment. It was the most intricate piece of metal work the boy had ever seen.

"This is extraordinary," he said. "Does it...?"

He was about to ask if it moved, but he never got to finish the question because at that very moment the automaton song thrush did, in fact, move. Its mechanical wings lifted from its body, its head began to turn, and its feet stepped up and down on Joshua's hand. The boy let out a great laugh. The bird was moving so authentically, it almost seemed alive.

But then it gave a little cough as though something was caught in its gullet. This was followed by another cough, which prompted Joshua to lean in closely and take a look in the bird's mouth. That's when the automaton gave an almighty cough and blew out a cloud of concentrated toxic green fog that billowed into Joshua's mouth and eyes and nostrils.

Magda jumped. "Oh my goodness!"

"Hmm," said Jude.

They watched as Joshua began to cough...and cough...and cough. He coughed so hard his eyes were the size of eggs and his skin went as green as an apple freshly plucked from one of the trees in the garden. Then he collapsed to the floor and lay still and silent as the song thrush tucked its wings into its sides and closed its tiny eyes.

Magda rose slowly from her chair, leaning to look at the boy without actually moving closer to him. "Is he dead?"

Jude glanced at her. "The boy or the bird?"

"The boy, silly!"

"I should think so," said Jude, going back to staring at the body on the floor.

"Will we be off then?" Magda asked.

"We'd better, my love. We have a long journey back to No Man's Landing. I hope we can be in Evercity before tomorrow evening. I want to make sure we're there when the Emperor hands out his rewards."

"The Emperor? You mean the Great Engineer."

Jude turned to look at her again, and stared into her eyes a long time before he answered. "No, my love. I don't."

Jude made his way to the grand front doors and pulled the lever, but as they slid open there was a sudden commotion from the back rooms of the manor. From down the long hall beside the stairs came the butler, flustered and upset.

"Master Joshua! Master Joshua!" he shouted.

"I'm afraid Master Joshua has taken ill," said Jude, blocking his way. "Is there anything we can do?"

"We've received a bird from Evercity!" The butler rung his hands as he spoke. "The Great Engineer has been usurped. The city is overrun with automaton forces and the Engineer's apprentice has taken the throne!"

"Is that so?" Jude's eyebrows went up, but his voice didn't change, and he calmly scratched at the side of his face before turning to Magda. "Come, my love, there's not a moment to lose. Aethasia has fallen at last."

CHAPTER TWO

IN THE DEEPEST and most disorienting part of the night it was difficult for Barthian Epistlethwaite to know which of the three noises had awakened him first: his father's sickly cough in the next room, the scrape of automaton boots on the cobblestones outside his window, or the many clocks on the shelves of the timekeeper's workshop, all of them ticking in tandem…but all of them ticking out of time.

Barthian propped himself on one elbow, squinting at his surroundings as the last images of his dream still flashed in his mind. It was a different kind of workshop, far away, and nothing like the timekeeper's hut. There was fog, and lots of it, and so many automatons, and the people who lived and worked there were sad, and dirty, and old, and hopeless. But he had found a way out. A cupboard, and a hole in the wall, and a tunnel that seemed to go for miles and miles. Up ahead there was a light, and Barthian was crawling towards it, getting closer and closer but never reaching the end, as his breath began to give out and the tunnel got narrower, narrower…

And then the dream ended. Every time. It didn't matter whether Barthian woke at six in the morning when the sun was starting to rise in the west, or whether, like now, he was woken in the middle of the night, his dream was always the same. Barthian never made it to the light.

From the next room, his father's cough came loud and painful, and came from so deep in his chest that sometimes it was all he could do to catch his breath. It rolled like thunder through the cottage as the watchmaker struggled to take in air, and then there was silence, a long silence during which Barthian wondered if his father had died. But then, as always, he coughed and spluttered.

It was a terrible sound that made Barthian feel helpless, especially since the clocks that the people of Aethasia had brought to them to repair were piling up around the workshop while his father lay in his sick bed. Barthian did what he could to keep up, but more people than ever were bringing their timepieces.

Clocks, watches…anything that ran on clockwork. They came from far away, well beyond the town of No Man's Landing, from places Barthian had never seen, and each person had the same complaint: Their timepiece didn't tell the right time.

There was another scrape of metal against stone outside the window of the workshop. The shutters were closed but even so Barthian knew that something, or someone, was there, trying to look in. It could only be one thing, because during curfew no one dared to walk the streets of No Man's Landing for fear they would be captured, or even shot.

The automatons that patrolled the streets day and night had grown fidgety and watchful in recent times. Something was wrong. Every day, Barthian heard new stories of someone or other who had been taken without warning, or fired upon in the streets for nothing more than running too fast, or passing too closely to a patrol. For his part, Barthian tried to keep to himself. He was too busy to stray far from the workshop, but when he did he made certain it was during daylight hours before the curfew was imposed, and he kept well clear of the patrols. So the sound of a dopey Troubleshooter at his window worried him. What did it want? Who was it looking for? What if it wasn't a Troubleshooter, but something more dangerous, like one of the Pacifiers, or even an Autofficer? Was it interested in timepieces…or was it spying on Barthian and his father, Germain?

Barthian lay down again and closed his eyes. He told himself to sleep, to fall back into the dream and perhaps even reach the light at the end of the narrow tunnel. But it was no good. The coughs from his father's room persisted, and the automaton was still at the window... but the thing annoying him the most was the sound of the clocks.

It wasn't the tick-tock of clockwork that keeping him awake. Barthian loved the sound of clockwork—it was the most comforting sound in all of Aethasia, like hearing the sound of his own heartbeat. There was nothing more perfect, or more reliable, than clockwork.

But that was the point. That was the very thing keeping him awake. There was something wrong with all the clocks, and it had to do with clockwork itself. He raised himself on his elbow again and listened, intently. He'd learnt as a small child, watching his father work from sunrise to sunset, how to truly listen to a timepiece to understand it, to diagnose its faults and figure out what it needed to be made right again. He would stand for hours watching the timekeeper, who stood with his ear raised towards the thatched roof as if listening for a distant ship.

Then a look would come over his face, which Barthian came to know was a look of discovery, of understanding. His father was never happier than at those moments, when he'd solved the puzzle and knew what he had to do. And now, Barthian had the gift. By the age of ten he'd been able to listen to the inner workings of a timepiece and almost visualise what was wrong. But as he lay there on his mattress of straw in the early hours of the night, with his ear cocked to the shelves of the timekeeper's workshop, he just couldn't figure it out. What was wrong with Aethasia's clocks?

Barthian got up and felt his way to the workbench. He felt for the candle and flint and lit the wick, and its yellow light filled the room with shifting shadows and a warm glow. There was a scurry at the window as the automaton backed away, then a clanging of metal boots against the cobblestones, fading away down the street. Barthian took a small clock from the shelf and placed it on the workbench.

"If I can't sleep, I may as well do my job," he muttered, and set to work on the clock, hoping today would be the day he finally came up with a solution. He was only fourteen years old, but when it came to timepieces he was determined to master every problem.

Even this one.

❦

Sunlight poured into the workshop through the open shutters when a hand upon his shoulder woke Barthian, who had fallen asleep at the workbench with a clock in pieces before him. He raised his head to see his father standing behind him, his cough easing at last. Germain Epistlethwaite chuckled and pointed at Barthian's face. Barthian brushed his fingers across his face and found a cog stuck to his cheek.

"Working late again, Bart?" Germain asked.

Barthian yawned and stretched. "Working early. I couldn't sleep."

"My fault, sorry," his father said, holding up his hands in mock surrender.

"Not just you. It's the clocks—it's time we worked out what was wrong with them."

"It is indeed," his father agreed, and scratched his beard as he looked around the workshop at the hundreds of clocks awaiting repair.

The workshop was a tiny space, but it was Barthian's most favourite room in the world. Not that Barthian had seen much of the world—as far as he knew he had never been anywhere else.

Because the workshop was small it was full of clutter: all the timepieces waiting to be fixed placed around the shelves, Germain's tools, Barthian's tools, and Barthian's little straw bed which he pushed back beneath the bench during the day.

There was one bay window that looked out onto the streets of No Man's Landing. Right across the square was Germain's oldest friend, Quinby Crabb, and his fishmonger shop. During the day the smell of his produce wafted into the timekeeper's workshop and made Barthian and his father very hungry indeed.

That didn't mean the fish was always fresh—far from it. Nothing much in Aethasia was ever fresh these days, because all the good stuff went to Evercity to be gobbled up by the imperial court and the wealthy guilds who did the Emperor's bidding. Even so, Quinby Crabb's fish was still too costly for what Germain and Barthian could afford. But that didn't stop them imagining what it would be like to cook a lovely fish broth, or a fish pie, or potato fish cakes, or fish fritters.

"What should we cook today, Barty?" Germain said, his nose twitching at the odour coming in through the space beneath the door.

"Hmm," Barthian pondered. "How about a chowder?"

Germain's face lit up. "A chowder! Do we have the ingredients?"

"Let's see," Barthian said, imagining that he was opening a pantry cupboard filled with spices and buttermilk and fresh herbs. "We have everything but the fish."

"Sorted, then," said Germain. "I'll be right back," and he began to walk on the spot, pretending that he was heading out to do the shopping.

They both laughed, which is how they got through the day, knowing all they would eat for breakfast, dinner, and supper would be oats with a little water. On the odd occasion, Quinby Crabb would come over at the end of a day and give Germain what fish he couldn't sell, and which Mrs. Crabb didn't fancy. Other times they might receive old vegetables as payment for fixing up a broken timepiece, and Germain would boil up a vegetable broth fit for the emperor himself.

That wouldn't happen today though, because they hadn't fixed a clock for days. But they couldn't complain, since both father and son knew there were many Aethasians worse off than they.

"Oh, that reminds me!" Barthian exclaimed, slipping off his stool.

"Where are you off to?"

"I promised Nelly some oats. I'll be right back."

"Wait, wait!" Germain called as Barthian ducked into his father's room and rummaged for a small bag of oats in the little food pantry beneath the bench and basin. "I've run out of tonic." He rubbed his chest. "Make sure you pay Lukas a visit for me…and make sure you're not seen."

"I will," Barthian said, but he was more concerned about getting oats to Nelly and her family before breakfast. Not that his father's tonic wasn't important—it was vital! Without Lukas's special medicine his father's lungs would stop working because of the fog-rot that had set in, what his father called the green lung. His father owed Lukas his life.

But first things first. Barthian hurried from the workshop and crossed the square, aware that he was risking drawing attention to himself by moving too quickly. As he scurried, his feet kicked up the green fog that lay like mist in the woods over the cobblestones of the town's streets, a perennial reminder that the emperor ruled every inch of Aethasia and subjugated its citizens with the fogtech that had come to dominate their lives.

As always, the automatons patrolled the streets. Troubleshooters patrolled in pairs because they were less heavily armed and easier to overpower. The more heavily-armed Pacifiers liked to stand on street corners, surveying the townsfolk as they hurried by, and occasionally stopping them for interrogation. There was even the odd Bombardier on patrol today, a foreboding automaton that bore heavy armour plating and could fire explosive artillery capable of destroying a whole building. Barthian had seen it happen. It was only this last Coronation Day that a patrol had tracked a fugitive into the heart of the business district and trapped him in the warehouse of Obadiah Copperwright & Sons. The blast from the Bombardier had taken down the entire front wall of the building and the shockwaves had almost blown Barthian off his feet from yards away. If ever he'd been tempted to mess with the emperor's troops, that day put him off forever.

Nelly's home wasn't far away. The urchins lived on the other side of the canal from the business district, because a good urchin is never far from where the coin is made. The urchins were the poorest of the poor, and in the new Aethasia there were more poor than ever. They clustered together in the Urchins Grotto, hoping that their neighbours, the merchants, might share their goods with them out of the kindness of their hearts.

That may have happened a long time ago, when fewer citizens struggled, but it didn't happen much anymore. There wasn't a lot of kindness left in Aethasia, not even in Evercity, which used to be the beacon of peace and prosperity throughout the entire land. No Man's Landing was a long way from Evercity, and even the merchants found life tough. But even the poorest of the town lived in relative luxury compared to the urchins. And among the urchins, they didn't come much poorer than Nelly and her family.

Nelly's house was nothing more than a small, corrugated iron shack leaning against a rundown building in what was once the thriving heart of the grotto. She had lived there with her mother and little sister since her father Phineas, a metal worker, was taken by the Emperor to the Fogworks years ago. He had not been seen or heard of since.

Barthian couldn't imagine what life would be like without his father. Nelly used to visit the timekeeper's workshop every other day asking for food, or coin, or both. Barthian would give her what they could afford or spare, and when her mother's ill health forced her to stop venturing out and stay home, Barthian had started making the trip across the canal to take them food instead. Nelly was his best friend. Apart from his father, she was the most important person in the whole of Aethasia to him.

"How are we today, Mrs. Lambkin?" Barthian asked, pulling back the curtain that hung over the doorway of the shack.

"Better for seeing you, Master Epist…Epsil…Epith…"

"It's Epistlethwaite, mother," said Nelly, gently.

Barthian smiled. Mrs. Lambkin had never been able to say his name…but she had never stopped trying.

"How's your father, my boy?"

"He isn't well, Mrs. Lambkin," Barthian said. "He still has the coughs."

"That nasty fog-rot," she said. Then she turned to Nelly. "If the cold doesn't kill us, the fog-rot will."

"'You mark my words,'" Nelly quoted.

"Exactly!" said her mother.

Barthian heard a small cough coming from the corner of the shack, where Nelly's little sister was huddled beneath a pile of rags to keep warm. Mirabella was rarely well, but the cough was more to get Barthian's attention, because Bella was sweet on him.

"How is Mirabella today?" Barthian asked. He was as fond of the little one as she was of him.

"She's improving, a little," Nelly said. "But slowly. She'll be okay. She's just being…" Nelly lowered her voice to a whisper. "…dramatic."

Mirabella suffered like Barthian's father, though not from the fog-rot. The cold and the damp made her ill, and when he could, Barthian brought a lump of coal so the Lambkins could light a small fire and warm up the shack. Their little shelter was nothing to look at, but it could get quite warm if the curtain was kept tight across the door.

"She's lucky to have you," Barthian said to Nelly, softly so that Mrs. Lambkin wouldn't hear. "I brought some oats. It isn't much."

"You're a sweetie," said Nelly, and gave Barthian a kiss on the cheek. The cheek immediately flushed red, which always made Nelly laugh. As always, Barthian walked away from the shack with his head in the clouds as he heard mother and daughter both laughing. He suddenly felt like whistling—no tune in particular, because music was banned across Aethasia by imperial decree. But it was a happy tune, completely made up and straight from the heart. He was still whistling as he strolled towards the square and home, completely forgetting that his father had asked him to run an errand.

"Whoops," he said, remembering, and turned on his heels to head to Lukas' place. But that's when he saw the small commotion outside the timekeeper's workshop, where a patrol of Pacifiers stood guard while a fearsome-looking officer in an imperial uniform and mechanical exo-skeleton rapped on the front door, demanding to be let in.

⁓

"I am Overseer Grimm," the man in the exoskeleton announced, "and I have come about a watch."

Barthian had squeezed past the patrol and was standing beside Germain in the workshop, where Overseer Grimm and one Pacifier, whose artillery arm was leveled at chest-height in sentry mode, were standing by the door to Germain's room. The workshop had never felt so crowded.

Despite being fourteen, Barthian was the size a normal ten-year-old should be; his father had been tall and broad once, but the fog-rot had made him small and feeble. In comparison, Grimm towered above them both. He wore the official uniform of an officer from the imperial court in Evercity, but the outer mechanism was unique. It was con-structed from polished steel and consisted of pipes and metal supports, with brackets at the epaulets on his shoulders and on his elbows, and great cuffs on the wrists, as well as a weaponised gauntlet on his left forearm. His legs had supports too—pistons that ran the length of his shin, and great metal boots like those worn by the automatons. His knees looked artificial, and Barthian wondered whether he had legs at all, or whether he was half automaton.

If the rumors Barthian heard about Grimm were true, the overseer had willingly undergone fogtech conversion to be more like an automaton, and more dependent on fog. That was crazy! Barthian sneaked a glance at the collar around Grimm's neck. There were pipes that appeared to enter his throat. That would explain the ventilation sounds coming from the unit on his chest, and the entire contraption, exoskeleton and all was powered by a fog boiler on his back. It surrounded Grimm with a constant green cloud, as the fog escaped from ventilation valves throughout the exoskeleton.

He wore special lenses over his eyes that appeared to be embedded in his skull, and only the faintest glimpse of his actual eyeballs could be seen through them. His shaved head and sharp moustache and beard made him look fierce and uncompromising. Everyone in No Man's Landing had heard stories of the cruel and cold-hearted commander of the Isle's fog mines. But this was the first time Barthian had ever laid eyes on the fanatic.

Grimm took a fob watch from a pocket in his tunic. The case was made of gold but the face of the watch was creamy white pearl. Embedded in the face were numerals carved from a beautifully honed purple crystal. Barthian had seen nothing like it.

"It was a gift—from the Emperor himself," Grimm warned.

He handed the watch to Barthian's father, who took it nervously and held it as though it might leap from his hands and fall to the ground at any moment. Germain turned it over and showed it to Barthian, who read the inscription on the back: "To my beloved apprentice, G.E."

"The letters G.E.," Germain said. "They're not the Emperor's initials."

"It was first a gift *to* the Emperor," Grimm snapped, "who then gave it to me."

"And what's the problem with it?" Germain asked.

Grimm gave a condescending snort. "That's for you to determine!"

"It doesn't appear to be broken." Barthian's father stifled a cough.

"It is…slowing down," Grimm said.

"Have you wound the crown?"

Grimm's hand flew from his side and struck Germain across the jaw, so that he spun and stumbled onto the workbench.

"Father!" Barthian shouted, and rushed forward to help. Germain held him at arm's length and turned his head away, but not soon enough to keep Barthian from seeing the blood oozing from his mouth. "You're hurt!"

"It's okay," Germain whispered. "No fuss, son. He meant no harm."

Grimm stepped closer. "I have no patience for insolence…" He suddenly paused, staring down at Barthian, and a wrinkle appeared between his eyebrows. "Where have I seen you before?"

"You haven't seen him anywhere!" Germain barked, raising himself upright from the bench and wiping his mouth.

But Grimm wasn't convinced. With his other gloved hand he held Barthian's chin, studying his face.

"Don't you touch my boy!" Germain ordered.

Grimm held up a finger, cautioning Germain not to interfere before continuing his examination of Barthian. "You look remarkably familiar," he said. "You remind me of…" He didn't complete his thought. Instead, he took a step backwards, and looked around the workshop.

"I expect you to give my watch your full attention. Priority one. I will return tomorrow. If it isn't fixed, it's the Fogworks for both of you."

"You're expecting too much!" Germain protested, but Grimm was having none of that. He strode from the workshop with his Pacifier right behind him.

Barthian reached out to help steady his father, who suddenly slumped against the bench.

"I'm all right," Germain said, feebly patting Barthian's shoulder. "I would have taken him on if you hadn't been here."

Barthian wanted to laugh at the thought of a sick old man challenging Grimm.

"I don't know what we're going to do about this watch though,"

Germain said, gesturing at it lying on the work bench. "I can't even see what's wrong with it."

"I can!" Barthian said.

Germain's eyebrows went up. "I'd love to hear it."

"It's the same problem that's affected all these timepieces," Barthian said, looking around the workshop. "If we fix one, we fix them all."

Germain shook his head. "I still don't see it."

"They're slowing down," Barthian said. "Every one. No matter how much we take them apart and put them back together again, no matter how much we wind them up, they keep slowing down, but in perfect timing with all the other timepieces...as if every clock in Aethasia is grinding to halt."

"Which means ..."

"We can't fix Grimm's watch, because someone has designed them all this way. The question is, who?"

"That's the *first* question," Germain corrected, stroking his beard again.

"What's the second?" Barthian asked.

"The second question is: Why?"

CHAPTER THREE

FATHER AND SON worked side by side throughout the day after the visit by Overseer Grimm. They spent the hours pulling timepieces apart and putting them back together again, but found no answer to the mystery of why Aethasia's clocks were slowing down, and consequently no solutions either.

Barthian watched his father closely as they worked. Nothing gave him more joy than seeing him disassemble and reassemble a beautiful timepiece with the care that only a master could give. But this time it was overshadowed by Barthian's concern about Germain's weakening state following the blow from Grimm. He knew Germain did his best to ignore how poorly he felt, and that he was keen to find a solution before the day was out...before Grimm returned on the morrow.

Before dismantling anything, they had tested Barthian's theory that every clock was slowing down at the same pace. It didn't take much time at all to prove that he was right. None of the clocks were keeping perfect time, but they were all keeping imperfect time together. Not all the hands of the timepieces around the workshop were in the same position, of course, but after observing them for a brief time they concluded every clock had the same problem.

"Well spotted!" Barthian's father said, when the problem was no longer in doubt. "Now we just have to figure out why, and what we can do about it."

"I still don't understand how it could have happened," Barthian said. "Not all of these clocks were made by the same timekeeper. How could they all have the same fault?"

Germain chuckled. "I've been wondering about that too. But I'm curious: Why do you assume it's a fault?"

That was simple. It was a fault because that's what everyone who brought a clock to the workshop called it. But was it a fault if it was part of the design? That didn't make sense though. A clock's purpose was to tell the right time. It wasn't much use to anyone if it couldn't do that.

Germain smoothed the beard on his chin. "There is one explanation," he said, staring into the distance. "Maybe we've been thinking about clockwork the wrong way."

Barthian frowned, studying Germain's face for clues to what he could mean. How could they have been thinking about time the wrong way?

"Clockwork is clockwork," Barthian said. "Time is...well, it's just time!"

"What if time is something else? What if it's a sign?" Germain picked up Grimm's watch. "Did you see the initials?"

"G.E." Barthian said. "Who is it?"

"There was only one G.E. who could call the Emperor his apprentice."

Barthian waited for his father to say more, but Germain had a sudden coughing fit. He coughed so hard that he had to go rest, while Barthian continued to work on the timepieces in the workshop.

"Did you get some tonic from Lukas?" Germain called from the other room once the coughing had finished.

Barthian gasped. "I forgot! I was about to head there when I saw Grimm at the door. Should I go now?"

"No, not now," his father said. "I have enough for one more night. You can go in the morning."

But Barthian struggled to focus on the timepieces after letting his father down like that. When he couldn't stand it anymore, he took an empty bottle from one of the workshop shelves and put it on his mattress. If he slept with it, the empty bottle would remind him about the medicine in the morning. Without the tonic his father would get seriously ill, and that's the last thing either of them needed when there was such an urgent mystery to solve.

When his father emerged from his brief rest he looked better. The colour had returned to his cheeks and there was a spark in his eye.

"I feel like a fish pie," he said, smiling.

Barthian smiled too. "We've done this already!"

"No, not the imaginary kind, the real kind! Let's go fishing!"

"Fishing? But we have so much to do. Grimm will be back in the morning and if we haven't fixed his watch—"

"It's not a problem we can solve in the workshop," Germain explained.

Barthian frowned. "But you always say everything can be solved in the workshop!" It was the reason neither of them had many friends. Their whole life had been about the workshop and the predictability of clockwork mechanisms and the surety that pulling something apart would always produce a solution.

"Not this problem." Germain shook his head. "This problem demands that we go down to the Pool of Stars and let our minds wander for a while."

Barthian felt his heart speed up. "Seriously?"

"I'm serious. Let's go there right now. It's just what we need."

"But..." Barthian glanced back to the fob watch lying on the workbench. "Grimm's watch..."

"Bring it!" said his father. "Put it in your pocket and bring it along. We'll be back before curfew. The watch will be quite safe with you."

Barthian was suddenly more aware of the smells wafting over from old Quinby Crabb's stall, and the thought of seeing the ocean and sneaking into the Pool of Stars felt like the perfect end to a difficult day. It was the one place in all of Aethasia where he felt completely safe. It was the place of his best childhood memories, where he and his father escaped to when they needed to talk, and to listen to one another, and to remind themselves that Aethasia was not all cruelty and poverty and fogtech, but a place of beauty and dreams.

Barthian slipped Grimm's watch into the pocket of his breeches and fastened the button. Then he grabbed their fishing poles, which in truth were nothing more than sticks with string and hooks tied to the ends.

"Light the candle," Germain said, casting his eye over the workshop. "Just in case we return after dark."

"Father!" Barthian protested. "We can't miss curfew!"

"We won't, my boy," he said, but he had a cheeky smile on his face. "Best to be safe though."

As Barthian lit the candle and placed it in a safe spot on the bench, his nervousness at the risk of missing curfew was overridden by a giddy excitement that they were heading to the Pool of Stars.

❧

It was late afternoon when Barthian and his father made their way through the streets of the business district. In the town centre the old relic of the great engine stood as a memorial to a distant past—a past that no one was allowed to discuss in public spaces anymore. The great engine loomed over No Man's Landing, casting its shadow over the entire town.

Barthian's father had told him the engine once helped to push back the mist that used to cover the land in the ages before the fog was even discovered. Barthian always found it hard to believe, or at least hard to imagine. He had never known anything but the fog and couldn't picture being able to see the sky without the fog haze hanging in the air, or walking through the streets of No Man's Landing without the fog curling around his legs.

"I remember it so well," Germain would say, but always quietly and in a hushed voice, in case someone, or something, was listening at the window, which the automaton spies often did. "There was no fog back then, the air and the water were clean. No automatons, either. We were free."

"How did they keep order without automatons?" Barthian would ask.

"I'm not sure," Germain would say, trying to remember. "They didn't need to."

"How about the propaganda carts?" Barthian asked. The Emperor's message machines seemed to be increasing all over No Man's Landing in recent days. They spewed continuous messages of praise for the Emperor and the world he had created with his fogtech. The carts trundled though the town like little fat busybodies, plastering posters onto walls to remind the townsfolk who they served, and why he deserved their adulation and loyalty.

"No carts either," Germain said. "None of that carry-on. The town was full of music…not lies."

"What happened?" Barthian would ask. "How did everything change?"

But that was when his father always changed the conversation, and the question Barthian had asked for as long as his father had told his stories was never, ever answered.

They headed through the town square and Barthian threw a glance at the Emperor's statue as they passed. He had never met the Emperor, but his father said the statue was a perfect likeness, though he never did say where he'd seen the Emperor himself. If it was a perfect likeness then Barthian hoped he never met the ruler of all Aethasia, because the statue gave him chills with its arrogant stance, cruel sneer, and piercing gaze.

Down the steps beside the town's newspaper they went, doing their best to avoid the Troubleshooters patrolling the small port, and headed across the air docks where the mine bulker from the Isle hovered in port, offloading what must be the hundredth shipment of fogrock for the day. The rock was carted off along the rail tracks that weaved through the town. All day and all night the hoppers came and went, the sound of their trundling wheels the signature tune of No Man's Landing.

The noise of the hoppers could be heard from every part of the town, heading out of No Man's Landing to the wastelands, and to the Fogworks—Aethasia's main refinery of fogrock that doubled as a prison camp for opponents of the Emperor. Anyone who dared oppose him, or even speak out against him in public, or openly talk about the good old days of the Great Engineer, was sent to the Fogworks for years, working the furnaces, sorting the rock, fuelling the ovens. While that wasn't the only thing Germain didn't like talking about, Barthian had long ago learnt never to push Germain on that particular topic.

Beyond the docks they followed the rocky path down to the cliffs. The autumn air had turned chilly, but Barthian and Germain wore their long coats and wrapped themselves up tight against the cold as they followed the winding path down to the coves. The closer they got the more they could taste the salt from the sea spray on their lips and smell the seaweed baking in the sun on the beach. What a glorious assault to the senses, spoilt only by the ever-present fog at their feet and the sound of automaton boots hitting the stone path as another patrol rounded the bend ahead of them.

"Evening," Germain said, nodding to the officer.

"Halt!" said the Pacifier, as two attendant Troubleshooters stood silently behind him. "Curfew at sun down. Vacate this area by nightfall, or face the penalty." Its voice was synthetic, unfeeling, inhuman. And slightly stupid, Barthian always thought, as if they had no mind of their own. Which they didn't, because each and every automaton only ever echoed the will of the Emperor…much like many Aethasians.

"Yes, yes of course," Germain said, almost apologetically, and he and Barthian moved on quickly before the automatons decided to be nasty and cut their night short, which was always a possibility.

Eventually they came to a narrow cleft in the rock, and Germain led Barthian through a passageway to a small beach that faced the setting sun in the east. The fog was thinner here, and they could see, in the distance, the shores of the wastelands, and the billowing clouds of green fog above it, which spewed from the Fogworks day and night. Sometimes, when the wind headed towards No Man's Landing from the east, the fog cloud made its way over the ocean like a storm and smothered the town, and at those times Germain's cough was worse than ever, constricting his throat and choking off his lungs so that he could barely breathe at all.

Not tonight though. Tonight there was an offshore wind and Smuggler's Cove felt like a private piece of paradise.

Barthian never tired of coming to his father's favourite spot, and never tired of hearing the stories of his father's youth, when the cove got its name. There were never any smugglers in No Man's Landing, not real ones, at least not back in the days of the Great Engineer. But in the early days of the Empire, when the shock of being without resources or food or fuel became a cruel reality, the inhabitants of No Man's Landing learnt quickly that to survive they would need to scrounge and scavenge. Germain recalled in vivid detail the night a supply ship was wrecked in this very cove, leaving no survivors. Word got around that the beach was covered in treasure and the townsfolk, to a man, broke curfew to head down to the water's edge to recover what they could.

"You got a barrel of salted pork, eh father?" Barthian said, as they made their way to the southern end of the cove.

"I did," Germain said, for what must have been the hundredth time. "The best bit of washed up salted pork I ever found on a beach. Now, shhh."

Up ahead they could see the Combustonaut patrolling the beach outside the cave, its flamethrower extended outward, ready to fire. Pilot flames licked the muzzle and multiple fog-boiler units on its back glowed bright green in the late afternoon light. The Cumbustonauts were frightening automatons, larger and more combative than the units stationed in town. There was only one thing worse than a Combustonaut, and that was a Lasher, the largest of the units stationed in these parts of Aethasia, with long tentacle-like arms that cracked like whips. Germain said there was only one thing to remember when faced with Lashers, or with Cumbustonauts about to scorch the earth around you: "Run!"

But Germain didn't run. Not this time, not even as the Combustonaut marched awkwardly toward them, its towering frame and plated armour battle skirts waddling like a duck.

"Quickly!" shouted Germain, running *towards* the Combustonaut. "Someone is putting up posters denouncing the Emperor, in the pass back towards No Man's Landing!"

"What! Wait! What?" said the Combustonaut, and fired off a small jet of fog-fuelled flame in excitement. It scurried away towards the narrow pass.

"Come on, quickly!" Germain said to Barthian, and headed to the boarded up entrance of the cave. The secret was knowing which of the boards was loose enough to swing downward, so that both of them could climb through and into the dark tunnel. It was no secret to Germain though, who carefully replaced the board before they headed off into the dark confinement of the tunnel.

"Hopefully, that Combustonaut will be on a wild goose chase for the next hour or so," Germain said. "Plenty of time for us to have a feed and laze by the Pool of Stars."

~§~

Barthian knew it wasn't far before the narrow tunnel opened into the main chamber of the cave, but he always got just a little scared. He didn't like to feel enclosed and the tunnel reminded him of his dreams and how the air would be squeezed from his chest. The tunnel itself was low and narrow and there was no light at all, so they had to feel their way along the cold, wet rock. But it was worth it.

The tunnel opened up into a small cave, just a little bigger than the workshop. Around its walls were the long-forgotten crates and barrels from the same run-aground ship whose cargo the town's inhabitants stored in the hidden cave. At the back of the cave was a waterfall that tumbled gently from the opening in the clifftop up above, and at the centre was a pool, into which the waterfall streamed gently, stirring up the crystal green and blue of the Pool of Stars. At midday the sunlight would hit the water from directly above, reflecting from the water's surface and flashing around the cave like a chest of jewels.

Now, in the failing light, the water was dark and blue and looked like it might tunnel as far as the heart of the world. The truth was, the pool tunneled beneath the beach and opened up into the ocean in the rocks at the southern end of the cove. Barthian's father said that as a boy he and his friends used to enter the cave from the ocean side, holding their breath for two minutes or more as they swam through the underwater tunnel. Barthian felt short of breath just thinking about it.

"How about some fish?" Germain said, taking a fishing pole from

Barthian and sitting crosslegged beside the pool. Barthian collected the driftwood they had stored at the edge of the cave the last time they were here. He'd brought the flint from the workshop, and it took him no time at all to light a small fire that sent a shaft of smoke up to the top of the cave, which was open to the sky like a large chimney. The smoke blended with the fog and the mist from the waterfall, so they had no need to worry about anyone using it to find them.

Germain had caught his first fish before the fire was even properly ablaze. This was the best thing about the Pool of Stars—the curious fish just came swimming to the top. He caught another, then a third, in quick succession.

"Enough fish for supper, breakfast and dinner tomorrow!" Germain said, and he was right.

The smell of the baking fish filled the cave as the fire warmed the air as well as their hearts. It was like the inside of a clay oven once the heat took hold, and the warmth, and the smoke from the fire, and the sweet aroma of baking fish was enough to make them believe they were not in the Emperor's Aethasia at all, but their own version of a distant or future perfect world—one that was more like the Aethasia Germain remembered as a boy.

With their bellies full, they lay down beside the water, Barthian with his head resting on his father's belly, as they gazed up at the sky and watched as the first stars began to break through the haze.

"I will be up there one day, with those stars," Germain said.

"Not for a long time," Barthian corrected him.

"No, not for a long time."

"Tell me more about the old days, about how it all changed."

"Aethasia was perfect," said Germain, and Barthian could tell by the dreamlike tone in his voice that he was away with the stars already. "I grew up in a perfect world…unlike you, I'm sorry to say. I was almost twenty years old when the Emperor took the throne."

"How did it happen?" Barthian pressed him. "You never talk about it."

"The Great Engineer's apprentice…your Emperor," Germain began.

Barthian's eyes widened, but he forced himself to stay still and keep his breathing quiet. His father had never talked about this before!

Germain continued: "He organised a rebellion against the Engineer and stormed the court, shut down all the Great Engineer's engines and replaced everything with his own fogtech. Then came the automatons, patrol after patrol, taking the loyalists captive and guarding the streets, installing fog boilers everywhere and corrupting everything good that the Great Engineer had created."

"Why did no one stop him?"

"Some tried, but they were captured and taken away."

"To the Fogworks?"

Germain went silent, and Barthian worried he had pressed too far.

"Look at the stars, Barty," he said, after a while. "So many of them, each one showing itself at the time of its own choosing. Pinpricks in the firmament."

Barthian gazed up there too and watched more stars emerge as the sky began to lose its colour and the darkness began to deepen.

"The G.E. on the back of Grimm's watch," Barthian said. "It stands for Great Engineer? It was the Engineer's watch?"

"I believe so, yes," Germain said.

"I always thought the Great Engineer was just a story."

"Far from it," Germain said. "The whole world of Aethasia is only here because of the Great Engineer."

Barthian rolled to one elbow to look at Germain's face. "But no one ever talks about him? If he was so important, why does everybody think he was just make-believe?"

Germain stared silently at Barthian for a long time, his jaw muscles moving ever so slightly, before he spoke. "The Emperor made a rule that no one could speak his name."

"What happened to him—to the Great Engineer?" Barthian asked.

"He fled during the usurping," Germain said, "and no one knows where. Some people think he died, alone, and in shame. Others say he went far away."

Barthian leaned closer and lowered his voice. "What do *you* think?"

Germain's eyes drifted from Barthian's face to the cave opening above them, as though he was thinking of the old days. "I think he is close. And I think he's just waiting for the right time to return. And I think the slowing clocks are a sign."

"A sign? A sign of what?"

"Think about it!" Germain raised his head and met Barthian's eyes again, sitting up far enough to gesture with his hands. "What's the one thing that remains from the days of the Great Engineer?"

Barthian shook his head.

"Clockwork!" Germain said. "Everything else—the great machines, the old tech, the pump houses along the River of Bones—everything the Great Engineer ever built that was good has gone, or has seized up, or been neglected or destroyed. Except our clocks. Clockwork is the only concession the Emperor made to the old Aethasia. Because he needs clockwork just like the rest of us. It remains our one and only link to those days, and to the Great Engineer himself. It's a symbol of beauty, and order, and precision and design. Time itself—it's the one constant we can rely on."

"And if every clock in Aethasia is losing time…"

"It means we're losing that one thing…if clockwork no longer functions as it did, then the Aethasia that once existed has gone forever, and there's no going back."

"Then how is it a sign?"

"Because if the Great Engineer is alive—and I believe he is—then he won't let that happen, I'm certain of it. He'll return to Aethasia before the clocks stop!"

"And if he doesn't?"

"Then it's true what they say: the Great Engineer is indeed dead, and Aethasia is lost."

Barthian's fish dinner felt unsettled in his stomach at the thought of there being no hope for a better Aethasia, and he returned to his previous position of reclining against Germain's side to think about what he's just learned.

As they watched, a great black shadow moved across the dark blue sky, the silhouette of a great airship.

Barthian sat up, staring. "What's that?"

"It looks like *The Lamentation*!" Germain said. "That's the only ship I know that is so big."

"The sky pirates?"

"Yes, the pirates—another consequence of the Emperor's new world. He lets them roam the skies and profits off their plunder."

Barthian realised the night sky was darkening quickly and curfew was approaching fast. "We have to leave before the Combustonaut returns," he said, scrambling to his feet. "We've already been here too long. We may not make it!"

"Let's stay here all night," Germain mumbled, and Barthian saw too late that he was already nodding off.

"Father!" he shouted, though not so loud that the Combustonaut would hear him. "Father!"

"Just let me have a little snooze," Germain moaned.

Barthian rocked his shoulder, tapped him lightly on his bearded cheek, and even splashed water in his face. "We have to go!"

Germain's eyes suddenly looked more awake, and he suddenly looked anxious himself. "Yes, yes," he said, struggling into a sitting position.

Out in Smuggler's Cove there was no sign of movement—the Combustonaut hadn't returned. Father and son retraced their steps along the beach and out from the cove, then along the narrow pass through the rocks. After pausing to listen for automatons, they set out on the path back towards No Man's Landing.

"HALT!" commanded a robotic voice from behind them, and they froze. "Violation of curfew is a crime against the Emperor!"

"We have a few minutes yet!" Germain insisted.

"Negative," answered the Combustonaut. "Violation has occurred."

"That's not true," Barthian said. He held up Grimm's watch, which showed there were several minutes to curfew.

The Combustonaut had no idea it was running slow, and stared down at the watch in confusion.

"Hand over your timepiece!" it ordered.

"We can't do that!" Germain said, moving between his son and the automaton.

"Final directive: hand over your timepiece!"

"The timepiece belongs to Overseer Grimm," Germain tried to reason. "I am the watchmaker, and I am fixing Overseer Grimm's timepiece."

"What is the nature of the problem with the timepiece?" the automaton asked.

"It's running slow," said Barthian's father, and instantly paled as he realised he had given the ruse away.

"Under arrest!" the automaton barked.

Barthian had been eyeing a large rock near where he was standing, and chose that moment to lunge for it, snatch it from the ground, and fling it at the automaton's head, knocking it backwards, just a step or two, but enough to put it off its guard.

"Run, father!" Barthian shouted, grabbing Germain's hand and fleeing down the path into the darkness.

The automaton wasn't done with them, though. It let out a jet of flame that caught Germain in the back and covered his coat and tunic with fire. That didn't stop them. They continued to run, and Germain undressed on the move, stumbling forward as he cast aside the burning clothes. They ran, ran for their lives, never giving any thought to what running in the night air, barely clothed and freezing, would do to poor Germain's chest. By the time they reached the end of the path and could see the docks, Germain had no air left in his lungs and he collapsed in a heap on the dirt.

"Father!" Barthian shouted again, taking his head in his hands. But this time there was no response. Germain stayed on the ground, his face to the sky, but his eyes firmly closed, and his body motionless and feverish. He was oblivious to the millions of stars that were filling the night sky above them...and to the Combustonaut about to kill them.

In the not-too-distant streets of No Man's Landing, the night patrols were sounding the alert and heading Barthian's way.

CHAPTER FOUR

GERMAIN AWOKE BEFORE the sun had risen the next morning, and his stirring woke Barthian, who had fallen asleep kneeling beside the bed. The colour of Germain's face had been so pale, and his skin so hot, that Barthian had been certain he would not make it. He knew he should get help, despite the curfew and the certainty that they would be arrested, but the fear of leaving his father alone had made him stay. So he spent the night cooling Germain's brow and forcing him to drink, as much as he was able, because Germain was delirious and feverish, and barely able to take a breath.

"Father!" Barthian said when he saw Germain's eyes open and scouring the room.

"Where am I?" Germain asked, and his voice was feeble and scared.

"We're home, at the workshop."

Germain blinked and looked again, scarcely believing what he was hearing.

"I had nightmares," he said. "Automatons, and fire."

"That was real, father," Barthian said. "We barely escaped."

"How did we...I remember...I collapsed!"

"Yes. I dragged you home, through the town."

"You dragged me? You're barely able to load the boiler with fogrock. How in Aethasia did you drag me home...and under curfew?"

"I don't know, to be truthful," Barthian said. "I kept to the shadows. The streets were thick with patrols. It took hours to reach home."

Germain reached out and placed his hand upon the back of Barthian's head and tousled his hair. "You are a special boy. This world does not deserve you."

Barthian could see the tears welling in his father's eyes. "Father …" he began, but Germain continued:

"It's true. You should have been born in the days of the Great Engineer. You would have been placed in his court and shown special favour. You might have stood at his right hand in the place of the Emperor."

Germain's teeth and fist clenched as he spoke, but the strain of the emotion sparked a fit of coughing that made the sweat pour from his forehead.

"I need my tonic," he whispered, his voice so frail that Barthian could barely hear him.

"I used the last of it to get your through the night, remember? I need to go and see Lukas."

His father nodded, slowly, and closed his eyes. "Go now," he whispered, and fell back into sleep.

Barthian slipped out of the workshop quietly, not only to avoid waking his father but also because it was still curfew and he didn't want to alert the patrols. He stayed in the doorway for a moment, scanning the streets for signs of movement, or the sound of steel on stone. Only when he was sure there were no automatons lurking in alleyways did he dare to emerge.

Lukas lived and worked near the racing pits, out the back of the business district near the canyons that led to the foot of the Old Mount, in an old warehouse that once had been a storage space for automatons. Lukas was a friend of the Emperor, or so Germain said. He was a mad inventor, an apothecary, a man of all-round science and spells who was often called upon by the Emperor for a new invention, or to fix something that his own engineers were not able to fix. That's why the Emperor left him alone to invent his gadgets and machines and experiment with plants and tonics, like a wizard holed up in his tower.

"Why are you friends with someone who supports the Emperor?" Barthian had once asked his father.

"I never said he supports the Emperor," Germain had said.

"But I thought…"

"Careful not to jump to conclusions," his father interrupted. "Lukas is a canny Aethasian, in more ways than one. He sees things in ways that no one else can, and he has more patience than anyone I know." And then, as if to emphasise his point, he said, "Lukas loved the old Aethasia with all his heart."

But Lukas wasn't so patient that he didn't get the grumps whenever someone woke him in the early hours of the morning, and he was none-too pleased when he came to the door, candle in hand, in response to Barthian's insistent knocking.

"What're you doing out here alone in the middle of the night?" he asked in his strange accent. Lukas was one of the northern folk who had migrated down from the hill country beyond the Old Mount in the early days of the Great Engineer. He was like a bear, with wild hair sprouting from his head and a beard that was just as wild, and a large girth that belied how much he enjoyed his food and drink—almost as much as his gadgets and engines.

"My father is sick," Barthian said. "Really sick. We need your help."

Lukas scanned the streets to make sure Barthian hadn't been followed, then ushered him inside.

"Be quiet about it, boy," he said. "I can't afford any more trouble."

Barthian let his eyes adjust as Lukas closed and bolted the door behind him, and stared with wide eyes and a gaping mouth at the state of the warehouse. Neat and tidy were not words anyone would associate with Lukas at the best of times, but what confronted Barthian was beyond the typical mess of Lukas' workspace. Tables were overturned, flasks were smashed, and bits of machinery were scattered across the floor.

"Mind where you go," Lukas said, picking out a path among the mess and perching on a high stool beside an upturned crafting bench.

"What happened?" Barthian asked.

"Oh, just a misunderstanding," the inventor said.

"With who?"

"Who else?"

Barthian's eyes widened. "The Emperor?"

"His lackey," Lukas corrected. "That villain, Grimm."

"Grimm paid us a visit yesterday too."

"Aye, well, he's on a roll. He was determined to leave an impression."

Grimm had left an impression, all right, Barthian thought as he looked around again. Grimm's automatons appeared to have smashed anything and everything they could get their hands on.

"What did he want?" Barthian asked.

"Just one thing," said Lukas. "The Aether Rose. I had two of them in the bell incubator over there—well, it used to be over there. That shattered glass is all that's left of it."

"The Aether Rose?" said Barthian, a cold knot settling in his stomach.

"Aye."

"You make Father's tonic from the petals of the Aether Rose."

Lukas nodded slowly. "Aye, laddie, I do."

"That's what I've come for. The tonic. Father's run out and I was meant to come for some yesterday."

"Well, laddie, that's too bad. Grimm took the rose and all the tonic I'd stored away."

"That can't be!" Barthian said. "Father needs it."

"I can make some more, laddie. Just as soon as the traders bring the roses from the Giant Seed Forest. They're due back in town in a couple of weeks. The Emperor has made it harder to get into the forest these days. He's building something special at the Echo Factory."

"No, you don't understand," said Barthian. His voice broke as he said it. "Father's dying. He needs the tonic now!"

Barthian and Lukas sat in silence for a short while.

"Sometimes that's all you can do once you've discovered there's no solution to yer crisis," Lukas explained. "The silence helps you think about all the other possibilities."

Lukas was good at that sort of thinking, and he scratched his head as he did it, making noises like "Hmm" and "Ugh" and "No, no."

"Why would Grimm want to take your Aether Rose?" Barthian blurted, unable to hold the question back anymore.

"That's easy, laddie," Lukas said. "Grimm holds the destinies of so many people in his hands, he's obsessed by it, almost as much as the Emperor. Now he holds your father's life in his hands as well."

"We need to fix that!" Barthian said, smacking his fist into his other hand.

"Yes, we would," Lukas agreed. "There's only one thing for it."

"What? Tell me. I'll do anything."

"You'll have to go to the Giant Seed Forest and fetch me a rose or two."

Barthian knew Lukas would come up with a solution...but he hadn't expected this.

"The Giant Seed Forest?! It's three days away!"

"Aye, it is, laddie...if you walk."

"How else would I get there? By airship?"

Lukas crossed his arms and nodded slowly. "That's one way."

"We don't have an airship. Or the coin to buy one. Or friends who can lend one to us."

"That's true, laddie. All of it. No doubt." More nodding.

"What then?" said Barthian. He had never been to the Giant Seed Forest. He had never been out of No Man's Landing, at least not that he could remember. But he knew how far the forest was. He also knew that the forest road was not the place for a fourteen-year-old boy, with its bandits and pirates and thieves and rogues and murderers. Not to mention the automaton patrols.

Lukas scratched his head some more. "I'm hatching a plan."

Lukas's eventual plan was this: Half a day's walk along the forest road was a small fishing village called Heron's Rush, where the River of Bones met the sea. The village was long-abandoned—it was years since that river had teemed with fish. But a friend of Lukas still worked a paddle-driven fog puffer from the river mouth to the old Everbright Quay, trading between the settlements along the way. A ride on the puffer would take two days off the journey.

"I'll send you with a note," said Lukas, and scrambled around for a quill and parchment to do just that. "Old Amos Cleverley's an eccentric old soak but he'll do the right thing. Over the years I've mended his little *Bitter Kiss* more times than I can remember."

"Bitter Kiss?"

"His puffer, laddie. His boat."

Lukas picked his way across the workshop to an upturned table. He rummaged among the broken gear scattered at his feet, mumbling to himself as he did so. Suddenly he stood upright with something in his hand, which he held up for Barthian to see.

"Found!" he shouted, and stomped back towards Barthian with a huge smile of satisfaction. "Here laddie, take this."

It was a hunting gauntlet, just like the ones Barthian had seen boys using in the woods, except in place of a catapult it had two small metal nodes and wires that ran beneath the leather strapping to a small gyro below the wrist.

"Try it on, make sure it fits," Lukas said. "It'll stand you in good stead on the road."

The cuff was made of leather thongs stitched at the wrist and the gauntlet slipped onto Barthian's forearm like a glove. Strapping secured the gauntlet around the palm of his hand, where a round, metal disc sat just above the ball of his thumb. The gauntlet was a little big, but secure enough.

"Now, aim at the table over there and hit the trigger with your fingers."

Barthian raised his arm as he was told, then aimed for the table and hit the palm trigger. Nothing.

"Try it again. It can be a little temperamental."

Barthian tried again, and this time a jet of steel-blue light sparked from the nodes and flashed across the workshop, exploding with a *CRAAACK* as it hit the workbench. Barthian gasped as Lukas chuckled.

"It's a little something I worked up with my pal, Irving," he said, with glee.

"Irving from the Grotto?"

"Aye, clever little chap he is. Bright future ahead, that boy has."

It was time to go. It was obvious to both of them that there was no time to lose, and the sooner Barthian left No Man's Landing the better. It was also obvious that it would be unsafe to travel alone.

"Have you anyone to take along for the journey?" Lukas said, while Barthian hesitated at the doorway to the street.

"There is one person," he said. Just the thought of taking Nelly on the road with him made Barthian feel more hopeful.

"Well, I'll wish you the best then laddie. I'll drop in to see your father and do what I can while you're away."

"Thank you, Lukas." Barthian adjusted the leather cuff of the gauntlet so that it was snug on his forearm. "Just one more question?"

"Absolutely, laddie."

"Do you think the Great Engineer is alive?"

"Whoa, laddie!" Lukas laughed. "Where did that question come from?"

"Just things that father was saying. Got me thinking."

"It's been a long time since anyone saw any sign of the Great Engineer around here," Lukas said. "We're not even allowed to speak his name!"

"I know," Barthian said. "But if he is alive...do you think it's possible he might return?"

"I can't say, laddie. But I will say this..." Lukas leant in closer and lowered his voice to a whisper. "If he does, I'll be the first to throw a party."

"Really?" Barthian asked.

"Absolutely! Listen son, the world became a dark and fearful place the day the Usurper forced the Engineer to flee. You have to remember something, particularly as you travel to the forest: the Great Engineer did a good thing when he made Aethasia what it is. It's hard to believe, I know, with things as they are. But even the very worst that the Emperor does, and the terrible things that villains like Grimm do, they can't wipe the goodness from Aethasia. So, yes—I believe the Great Engineer is very close. Will he return? I don't know. But for some reason, I've always had hope...hope that we'll see him one day and that he'll restore Aethasia to what it once was."

"Hmm," Barthian pondered. Lukas was right about one thing— Barthian couldn't imagine a day when things would be better; when the automatons had disappeared from the streets of No Man's Landing, or when everyone had food to eat and coin in their pockets. It was beyond what he could hope for.

He bid farewell to Lukas quietly—curfew was not yet over—then crept carefully through the streets, keeping close to the shop fronts and warehouses and cargo containers, slipping in behind stacks of barrels and crates, pausing in doorways, alleyways, and standing in the shadows beneath the awnings—whatever cover he could use to stay clear of the patrols, which marched right on past as he kept still and silent and invisible. He headed, not for home, but over the canal and into Urchins' Grotto. He couldn't travel all the way to the forest by himself, and Nelly was the one person he knew would go with him.

⤚

Nelly was asleep, huddled in a corner of her shack beside her mother and sister, when Barthian tapped on the door frame and opened the curtain. It was as cold inside as it was outside in the Grotto and Barthian realised again that no matter how hard he and his father found life in Aethasia, there was always someone who found it tougher.

"Nelly!" Barthian whispered. "Nelly, wake up!"

Nelly rubbed her eyes, yawned, and stretched her arms, then squinted at the silhouette of Barthian in the doorway.

"Barty?"

"I need your help," he whispered, to avoid waking Mrs. Lambkin. "Can we talk outside?"

Fire pots were burning throughout the Grotto day and night. The urchins congregated around the fires, did their cooking there, got warm together, and heated their pots to make tea. It's where they chatted, laughed, plotted, teased, dreamed and schemed. Nowhere else in No Man's Landing could people gather together like they did in the Grotto, because the Grotto was the one place the automatons rarely came. The urchins were utterly neglected by the Emperor, and mostly it was to their advantage. If any Aethasian wanted to scheme against the Emperor away from spying eyes, they only need come to the Grotto to do it.

Barthian and Nelly stood beside the fire, and he told her all that had happened since he'd seen her in the Grotto the day before. Nelly listened with a growing look of dismay on her face. But when Barthian came to outlining a strategy for the journey ahead, her head dropped.

"I can't," she said. "I'm so sorry, Barty. But how can I leave my ma? She needs me. My sister needs me."

Of course she couldn't, Barthian realised with sinking disappointment. Her family needed her as much as his needed him.

"I'm sorry," she said again, and reached for his hand. "There is still something I can do to help, though."

She led Barthian into the slums of the Grotto, where the streets were as narrow as the back alleys in the business district, and the houses so decrepit that they leant over like trees in a storm. The two of them weaved through the rubbish bins, crates, and junk that had been dumped on the street, all the way back to the darkest corner, and down a crumbling flight of basement stairs to a small doorway. The door was unlocked, because there was nothing in the Grotto worth stealing, so Nelly went inside. Four boys, slightly older than Barthian, sat at a small table drinking coffee and playing a card game.

"This is Salmon!" Nelly said, standing beside a boy with dark skin and matted, thick hair and a ring in the side of his nose.

"Salmon?" Barthian said. "Like the fish?"

"Solomon," Salmon said. "But no one says it proper. What can you do, eh lads?"

"You're from the eastern lands, over the horizon?" Barthian marveled.

"Years and years ago," Salmon said. "The oldies were refugees in the days of the Great Engineer."

"Great Engineer!" the three other boys mumbled together, like a chant. "May he return!"

Nelly got Barthian to repeat his story, and as he laid out what he needed to do, Salmon nodded thoughtful.

"I have travelled the forest road," he said, "all the way to Everbright Quay. There are dangerous places out west. Dangerous folk, too."

The others nodded, and Barthian's head dropped. It seemed he was going to have to take this journey alone.

"I will go with you," Salmon announced, standing up from the table. "Love me an adventure!"

Barthian raised his head, blinking in surprise. "Wait—you're coming?"

"Gear me up boys!" was Salmon's only reply.

"Gearing up" consisted of arming him with whatever they could lay their hands on, including a catapult hunting gauntlet, a long knife that he strapped to his leg, and a large hammer that he hung from his back. Salmon wore the leather strappings of the Horizon People, wound tightly around his arms and his torso. There were thicker straps around his legs, and he wore large boots he claimed to have stolen from a merchant somewhere. One of his gang gave him a pair of sky-captain's seeing goggles that he wore on his head in the pirate way. He was a formidable sight.

"The genuine article this," Salmon told Barthian, pointing to the hammer on his back. "A real live Breaker gave us this, eh, boys?"

The boys laughed.

Barthian gaped, the mere thought of the emperor's automaton death squad giving him chills. "Breakers never give up their weapons without a fight! You mean you actually took one of them on?"

"That's right, Tick-Tock," Salmon said, grazing Barthian's shoulder with his fist.

"Tick-Tock? Uh, my name's Barthian."

Salmon ignored him and called out a "Rightio!" to his gang in a farewell salute as he and Barthian left the basement hideaway. At the square, Nelly bid them a sad farewell, because there was nothing more she would like to do than travel the forest road with her friends. Then Barthian led Salmon through the business district to the timekeeper's workshop, to check on his father one last time.

"Father," he whispered, kneeling beside his bed again.

Germain opened his eyes and smiled. "You're still here?"

"I've been and come back again," Barthian said. "Listen to me carefully."

Barthian told Germain about Lukas and the tonic, and about Grimm's ransacking of the warehouse. Germain gripped his hand as

Barthian told him about the plan, and about Salmon and the Giant Seed Forest, and old Amos Cleverley, Lukas' river captain friend.

Germain's eyes welled, and Barthian realised they were thinking the same thing. For too many reasons to speak out loud, this could be the last time they shared such a moment.

"We should go before the sunrise!" Salmon said from the doorway.

Barthian leant on the bed to kiss his father on the cheek. Germain placed his hand on Barthian's back, and held him there.

"Don't go!" he whispered, feebly. "Too dangerous!"

But there was no choice—none at all. Barthian would happily face any danger in the whole of Aethasia if it meant keeping his father alive. He paused at the door, took one last look at Germain, whose eyes were closed, unable to bring himself to see his son depart. Barthian had packed as many of the oats as he thought he could while still leaving some for Germain, put them in a small sack, and slung it over his shoulder as Salmon checked outside for automatons.

Then they made their way out into the streets.

And there was Nelly, waiting in the shadows! She had a big coat over her plain dress and a stained, fraying cap on her head. On her feet were boots that were obviously too big.

"Mom said I should come along," she said. "Reckoned you boys couldn't do it without me."

"That's truth, that is, Chops!" Salmon declared. "Aint it, Tick-Tock?"

"The name's Barthian," Barthian reminded him.

"Not on this trip it ain't! Top secret! Code names only. I'm Salmon. She's Chops. And you're blooming Tick-Tock!"

"Fine," Barthian muttered. He had more serious things to be concerned about. "Whatever you say!"

So, the three of them set off together, creeping through the streets of No Man's Landing towards the west while the town woke to the dawn and the breaking of curfew, as the sun began to rise over the horizon—a horizon they had to reach before time ran out for Germain. As it climbed, the sun cast long shadows that looked like fingers reaching out towards them across the landscape—an ominous warning of the hazards they would surely face.

CHAPTER FIVE

OUT BEYOND THE western boundary of No Man's Landing, the forest road climbed gradually away from the sea, so gradually that Barthian didn't even realise they were climbing. At least, not until they looked down and saw the road winding over the rocky hills that rolled behind the town for miles and miles, gradually becoming the skirts of the highest mountain peak in the land, the Old Mount.

At their highest points, the hills became sparse, like moors, with low scrub and mountain goats, and rocky outcrops, with bubbling bogs in the valleys between them. To the left Barthian could see out over the sea, and behind him the green cloud of fog that sat over No Man's Landing day and night. It wasn't until now that he was in the hills that he could see how thick and soupy the fog really was, and the first time he looked back and saw it for himself, Barthian stopped to properly take it in.

No wonder his father was sick and unable to breathe. And no wonder the people of No Man's Landing had forgotten what it was to live outside the fog cloud, to breathe fresh air and grow good crops, and raise animals that were fat and healthy.

"It's so ugly," he said.

"You've never seen it before?" Salmon asked.

Barthian shook his head. "Never. Not from outside, like this." If it wasn't for his father, down there awaiting his return, Barthian knew he could keep walking forever, as far from No Man's Landing as his boots would carry him.

The three of them continued on, as the sun rose higher and the autumn day grew warmer. As they climbed the next crest they saw sails flying in the sky, like the massive kites Barthian had sometimes seen boys from No Man's Landing flying on the beach.

"Well, what do you know!" Salmon sprinted ahead, and Barthian and Nelly followed.

Over the other side of the hill in a small valley covered with low-lying green fog, was a large group of urchins, each one holding a long, thin pole that was fixed to a sail. Each sail had two poles, one on each end, and the urchins ran through the fog in pairs, collecting it on the sails like you might catch butterflies in a net.

"What are they doing?" shouted Barthian, running to keep up with Nelly.

"They're the fog catchers!" Nelly said, as if Barthian should know already. "They catch the fog in their nets to use in their burners back in the grotto."

As they got closer to the group, Barthian saw that the fog catchers were around his age, and they were indeed catching the fog in the sail-nets, then collecting the condensed fuel in old cans.

"Barthian, come meet Benny!" Salmon shouted.

Benny was the tallest among them, a swarthy urchin with a rugged face and wild hair. He stood as if ready to flee as Barthian approached, but as Salmon told Benny where they were headed and why, Benny broke into a smile and held out his hand.

"I never thought such a thing was possible," Barthian said, marveling as the urchins ran up and down the valley with their large sails, like ships on a foggy ocean.

"Urchins can't be loungers," Benny said, quoting the common Aethasian phrase. "If we don't catch the fog, we'll freeze. Our people can't afford fog rock or coal, so we have to be clever about it."

"It's amazing," Barthian said, suddenly wishing he could stay up there on that hill and help the urchins collect fog for their burners. But Nelly tugged at his arm to remind him that time was moving on.

"Would you like us to come with you?" Benny asked Salmon.

Salmon started. "To the Giant Seed Forest?"

"Why not? The gang is always up for an adventure! We've got weapons with us."

"The extra muscle would come in handy," said Salmon, nodding and rubbing at the beard he didn't have. "But no. The gang would draw too much attention. We need to get in and out of there undetected."

Benny's shoulders sagged, and he sighed. "Well, you know where to find us if you change your mind," he said to Salmon. "Or any other time!" he added to Barthian.

They bid their farewells, and Salmon led the way from the valley, up and over the hill towards their destination. On and on they walked as the afternoon wore on—uneventfully, for which they were very grateful. When they came across a rocky outcrop they would rest their feet a while, sitting in the cool shade of boulders that had sprung out from the moors with no rhyme or reason. If they came across a spring they stopped and cupped their hands to drink, and Barthian always marveled at how differently water tasted when it hadn't been tainted by bitter, rancid, fog-polluted rivers.

But for the most part, they walked throughout the morning, through wide tracts of moorland covered in cotton-grass and mosses, bracken and heather. The further they got from No Man's Landing, the clearer the horizon ahead of them became. In the far distance they could see the darkened strip of green woodland that swept up towards the north and the foothills of the Old Mount, which rose high in the distance off to the right, its snowy peak encircled by a ring of cloud. Beyond the woodlands the horizon shone in a strip of sparkling blue-white light, much like the light given off by his gauntlet.

"What is that?" Barthian asked, pointing.

Salmon followed his gaze. "In the distance? That's the Giant Seed Forest. That's where we're going, Tick-Tock."

"No, beyond that—the light beyond the woodlands."

"You mean the Snowmoors? That's as far as Aethasia extends. Further than I've ever been."

"And me," said Nelly, who was walking merrily enough over the moors even though she had whispered to Barthian earlier that her boots made her feet hurt.

"What's out there?" Barthian asked.

"That's where the Academy is." Salmon's voice was low and serious as he said it.

"The Academy?"

"The Academy Automicus, where they train the officers who captain the automatons."

"They really are everywhere," Barthian mused, struck by the Emperor's reach across every corner of Aethasia, from the Fogworks in the East where the automatons were designed and built, to the Academy in the West, where his battle bots were trained and deployed under the leadership of Aethasians who had sworn allegiance to him.

"Don't forget the Echo Factory!" Salmon said.

"Lukas told me about that. What is it?"

"It's the Emperor's boatyard in the middle of the Old Forest, where he makes his airships. It's a monstrous thing, a giant floating ship hidden by enormous trees, working day and night to build and repair his fleet. It's why the forest is defended by the Boomlands."

"The Boomlands?"

"Great floating mines, chained to the ground but ticking like bombs." Salmon made a big circle with his arms, indicating the shape of the mines. "They can detect any intruder, big or small, and they sweep down on anything that moves and…BOOM!" He flung his arms out, imitating the explosion.

Barthian stopped walking, gazing out at the distant forest. Across his mind flashed images of mines blowing them to bits, of automatons gunning them down, of their bodies being left lying where they fell with no one to bury them or care. What in all Aethasia made Barthian think he could take on the Emperor this way?

"I can't do this," he said.

Nelly's gentle hand touched his arm. "Barty?"

"This journey, I—I'm no hero. I can't do it. It's too dangerous—for all of us."

Salmon grabbed him by the arm.

"Keep moving, Tick-Tock," he said, pulling Barthian along. "Everyone gets the jitters."

"This isn't the jitters," Barthian argued, shrugging Salmon off. "It's accepting the truth."

"The truth?" Salmon shouted. "The truth has nothing to do with what you can't see, Tick-Tock. The truth is what you know!" He jabbed a pointing finger against his temple. "The truth is who you share it with." He pointed at himself, then Barthian, then Nelly. "The truth is what you do." He pointed in the direction they had been walking.

Barthian blinked, and looked hard at Salmon, suddenly aware of what he didn't know about this strange boy from the Grotto who was uttering such wise words. "Who *are* you?"

"My Ma always said, truth isn't out there, in those distant lands, or hidden monsters. Truth is up here—" Salmon tapped his head. "—in here—" He tapped his chest. "—and in here." He held out his hands. "The journey ain't over yet, Tick-Tock. It's barely even begun."

Salmon strode ahead, and Nelly took Barthian's hand in hers again.

"He's right," she said. "It's not time to give up."

"I know," said Barthian. "I just—oh no!"

"What is it?" Nelly asked, as Barthian struggled with the pocket in his breeches.

"Time!" He pulled Grimm's watch from his pocket and sunk to the ground. "I forgot all about it."

"What is it?"

"It's Grimm's watch, the one he asked us to fix. He's coming back to the workshop today. I have to take it back."

"What's wrong now, Tick-Tock?" Salmon shouted from up ahead.

"He's brought Grimm's watch by mistake! He needs to take it back."

"I wouldn't be doing that!" Salmon said, looking beyond Barthian to the path back towards No Man's Landing. He brought the seeing goggles down from his head and placed them over his eyes, adjusting the frames.

"You don't know!" Barthian cried. "My father's life depends on it."

"Your life depends on it too." Salmon pointed. "Look!"

Barthian turned and saw what Salmon was pointing at: a figure in the distance, hooded and dressed in black, tracing their path. He was still a long way off across the barren landscape, but even from this distance Barthian could tell that he was pursuing them...and doing so at pace.

Barthian gulped. "Is it Grimm?"

"Too hard to see," Salmon said, adjusting the goggles some more. "Grimm, or one of his officers. His secret police, I reckon."

"How long before he catches up with us?"

"You're the one with the watch. Thirty minutes? Maybe less?"

"Right then." Barthian scrabbled to his feet and put the watch back in his pocket. "Let's run!"

⸎

They ran until their legs gave out, which wasn't very far in truth. Running in No Man's Landing was dangerous for a number of reasons, so they didn't exactly get much practice. But they made it far enough to see that their path had brought them to the crest of the hills, and from there it began to drop away back towards the coast. More importantly, they could see Heron's Rush, the old fishing village at the mouth of the River of Bones. It was little more than a cluster of small, stone cottages, with a small jetty where the fishing boats once would have been secured. But there was no sign of life at all. No smoke from the huts, no fishermen on the water, not even a stray animal. And there was no sign of Amos Cleverley, the puffer captain.

They made it around an outcropping of rock and leant back against the rock face, taking deep breaths. Their legs were wobbly and weak and their heads were hot and sweaty. Still, they could see that the hooded man had gained on them, perhaps by more than half the distance. He was pursuing them relentlessly, taking great strides as he chased them along the path over the hills.

"No sign of him giving up," Salmon observed, watching the hooded man through the seeing goggles.

"No sign at all," Barthian gasped, barely able to take in the air he needed to recover for the run down to the river. It made him think

50

of his father, back home at the workshop, and he wondered whether Grimm had returned. He still felt bad about holding on to the watch, but he knew that he had to keep going, to ignore how badly he felt and, if he could, use it as a spur to keep moving. If only they weren't being hunted down by a hooded stranger.

"I'm scared," Nelly admitted.

Barthian put his hand on her shoulder. "I'm scared too. But we're still together. And the village is just there."

They set off again. Barthian's legs were so tired it felt like he was walking through wet sand. At least the path was heading downwards now, so his greatest fear was slipping on the stones beneath his feet and landing on his backside. This must be what the mountain goats felt like, picking a path through rocks and low scrub, stepping carefully and intentionally, but as quickly as they could.

As the path dropped towards the village they were hidden from the hooded man, which gave them at least some relief, albeit temporary. For the next little while Barthian tried to put him out of his mind and focus on the village and the race to get there.

Finally, the path entered the trees at the foot of the hills, and from there they emerged onto the coastal plain, where the ground became soft sand, with small dunes covered in beach grass and ferns and bracken. It felt like the final moments of a nightmare to Barthian—the fishing village almost within reach, a hooded man dressed in black in close pursuit…and the ground suddenly and unexpectedly so soft that they could barely make progress. He wanted to shout for help, but to do so would only alert their pursuer, not to mention frighten poor Nelly out of her wits. They just had to keep going, one…step…at a…time.

They reached the huts and collapsed with exhaustion beside the river, rolling onto their backs with their faces to the sun, which was high in the sky above them.

"Just a few moments to catch our breaths," Salmon said, taking charge. It had bothered Barthian, up on the hills, before they had spotted the hooded man, the way Salmon just assumed control.

But now…now that they were running from danger, he didn't mind so much that Salmon was barking orders. Salmon was older, after all.

Salmon had beaten a Breaker and taken their weapon. Salmon was tall and strong and had travelled this road before. Salmon had fled danger his whole life. So Barthian did as he was told.

"We need to look around," Salmon said. "Try to spot any signs of the boatman … or a position we can defend."

"He'll find us," Barthian said. "I know it."

"Then let's hurry."

There were seven huts in all, each one as rudimentary and deserted as the next. They found old fishing gear, such as line, and nets, and pots. In one hut they found evidence of a recent fire, an upturned crate for sitting on, signs of pipe tobacco, and the remains of a meal or two.

"Your man has been using this hut, Tick-Tock," Salmon said. "Hopefully he ain't too far away."

In another hut they found old rope and a sack, and thought quickly about trapping the hooded man somehow. Then just as quickly they realised that was a stupid idea—the hooded man would be too close too soon, and they wouldn't have time to set any kind of serious trap.

"Show me your weapon," Salmon said to Barthian.

Barthian had noticed Salmon eyeing the gauntlet along the way, and held up his arm.

"What does it do?" Nelly asked.

Barthian suddenly felt shy. "Well, it—it sort of…shoots lightning."

"Fog in the rock!" Salmon shouted, eyes wide and mouth gaping. "You kept that little gem quiet!"

"I've had no need to use it," Barthian said sheepishly.

"No need? Last time I looked we were being chased by Grimm's henchman."

"We can't go blasting strangers!" Barthian said, in truth unsure that he could really blast *anyone*, now that it came to it.

"I agree with Barty," Nelly said.

"In normal times, I suppose I might agree too." Salmon rubbed at the matted hair on his head as if it helped him make sense of things. "But these are not normal times."

"Still, I don't think—"

Barthian stopped as Salmon held up his hand and listened…then they heard it together: a not-too-distant sound, a familiar chug-chug-ging of a fog-powered engine, followed by the not-so-familiar churning of river water, as big paddle wheels propelled a puffer downriver.

"There's our boatman," Salmon said, clapping his hands. "We're riding our luck today."

They ran outside to see how far away the puffer was, but stopped dead in their tracks as the hooded man, his face covered by a black mask and his eyes shielded by goggles, his hands gripping two large and powerful pistols by his sides, stepped out from the closest stone hut and took up a position between them and the approaching puffer.

Nelly screamed, Salmon cursed, and Barthian...well, Barthian, without even thinking about it, raised his gauntlet at the hooded stranger and pressed the palm trigger as hard as he possibly could.

❧

The lightning flashed from Barthian's forearm but missed the hooded man, who pitched away to his left, back inside the stone hut. But the lightning did hit the doorframe and blow it apart, which in turn brought down the entire front of the hut, right down on top of the hooded man. That's what he assumed anyway, because the cloud of dust that billowed from the blast prevented him seeing anything inside the hut at all. But there was no sign of the hooded man anywhere.

"Here's our chance!" Salmon shouted, turning towards the river and waving his arms at the oncoming puffer. "Quickly! Tick-Tock! Chops!"

Barthian was rooted to the spot, filled with a sudden surge of guilt. Nelly grabbed his hand again and pulled him towards the river. Up ahead, Salmon had reached the jetty, where the puffer was manoeuvring in to dock. A large man with a bald and ruddy head stood at the rear of the boat, handling the rudder. He had on a big oilskin coat and a bright red kerchief around his neck. He threw a rope to Salmon, who quickly wound it around one of the bright yellow bollards.

"What in all Aethasia was that?" the big man shouted. Nelly and Barthian had run to Salmon's side, though Barthian kept glancing back, half hoping but also dreading to see the hooded man rise from the rubble.

"Some shoddy stonework, that's what!" Salmon shouted back.

"I'll say it's shoddy," said the man, who they assumed was Amos Cleverley. The name *Bitter Kiss* could be seen in flaky yellow paint on the side of the old puffer's hull. "Were any of you hurt?"

"Safe and sound," said Salmon. "But desperately in need of a ride."

"Oh, you are, are you? Well, I'm afraid there's no free rides today."

Barthian shook himself from his mild shock and dug in his pocket for Lukas's note. Cleverley took it and read it over with his small, porcine eyes. They were like little beads of glass, buried deep in his huge head, which was leathery from too much sun.

"So, you know old Lukas, eh?" he said, watching Barthian and the others suspiciously.

"He's an old friend," Barthian answered. "He's helping my father, who's very ill."

"Back in No Man's Landing?"

"Yes," Barthian said. "He's the town's timekeeper."

Cleverley shook his head. "Well, any friend of Lukas is a friend of mine."

Barthian breathed a sigh it felt like he'd been holding for days as an invisible weight fell from his shoulders. He even managed a smile. It didn't last long, however, because as Salmon made to climb onto the puffer, Cleverley stopped him with a typically large, leathery, and warty boatman's hand.

"Not so fast, dreadlocks!" he said. "There ain't no free rides on the River of Bones. Do you know how much coin it takes to fuel this little beast with fogrock these days?"

"But…the note," Barthian said, confused.

"Lukas asked me to give you fellas a ride. He said nothing about doing it for no coin." Cleverley held out his hand.

The trouble was, they didn't have any coin.

"What's it to be?" Cleverley asked. "We walking to the Everbright Quay, or we sailing up the river?"

Barthian turned away—he couldn't bear for the others to see the

54

disappointment and embarrassment on his face. But Salmon and Nelly came and stood by his side.

"Have you no coin at all?" Salmon whispered.

"Nothing," Barthian said. "Not even a gold tooth."

"What about that special watch in your pocket? Far as I could tell, that was coin enough."

"Grimm's watch?" Barthian's hand moved protectively over his pocket.

"Well, he ain't using it," Salmon reasoned. "And who knows, we might find some coin along the way and you can buy it back!"

Barthian shook his head and clenched the cloth of his pocket in his fist, gripping the watch even more firmly. He had seen Grimm up close, and couldn't bear the thought of being in his presence again, trying to explain how he'd given away his most precious gift to a puffer boat captain.

"That's it then," Nelly said. "Looks like we're walking."

"We ain't walking," said Salmon, getting loud. "It's too far. And too dangerous!"

Behind them, Amos Cleverley paced the deck of his puffer, one fist on his hip. "You fellas can cast me off if you've changed your mind," he said, stoking up the two-group double fog boilers on the back of the puffer. The engine chugged away beneath the boat as the boilers blew green fog every which way, which sent Cleverley into a coughing fit. "Righto then, I'll be off," he said, once he'd recovered.

Once again, Barthian was caught mid-decision, fully aware that the Giant Seed Forest was too far away to even attempt a walk, but too cautious to give away Grimm's watch. His indecision got a kick in the pants, however, when the rubble that had fallen upon the hooded man began to shift. Stones fell away from the heap and dust rose like clouds, as the cloaked but ragged figure slowly raised himself upright, arching his back and stretching his arms out wide. The pistols were still in his hands.

"Here's a gold watch!" Barthian blurted, turning and leaping onto the puffer before Cleverley could say anything.

"What's this?" the big man said, rubbing the watch face on his big, round belly before squinting at it with one eye.

"It's worth more than your little puffer and all the trade you'll do in a year," Salmon said, helping Nelly onto the boat. "And it's yours, if you get us out of here alive!"

"But who—what—where did that come from?" Cleverley said, pointing at the hooded man with a porky finger.

"He's from Overseer Grimm," said Barthian, urgently. "And he's after your watch!"

"Ohh, I see!" Cleverley said, and bounced into action.

"Wait, wait, the rope!" Salmon shouted, and leapt back onto the pier.

"Quickly!" cried Nelly. The hooded man leveled his pistols at the puffer, then let off a volley of shots. They whizzed overhead as all of them ducked, even Salmon, who was frantically unwinding the rope.

"That's enough of that!" Cleverley barked, lifting a rusty old rifle from the back wall of the boat and giving the hooded man a volley of his own. He backed the puffer away from the jetty as the hooded man took cover behind a hut, and as Salmon bounded back on board. But the hooded man reappeared again, running after them with his guns raised.

"You'll have to do better than that!" Cleverley yelled, firing again.

The hooded man returned fire, but again he missed the boat.

"Quickly!" Nelly shouted again.

"Don't worry, my dear!" Cleverley said, laughing. "He won't catch the *Bitter Kiss*, doesn't matter how fast the fella can run."

But the hooded man had stopped running and stood on the wooden jetty, arms hanging limp at his sides. Cleverley clasped Grimm's watch in his hand, raised it above his head, and shouted, "Give my best to Grimm!"

The *Bitter Kiss* chugged away upriver, ferrying them to safety. Salmon and Nelly raised their faces to the sun and smiled as the river breezes whipped their hair and faces. But Barthian sat alone in the cabin, thinking of the watch, unable to shake the feeling he had just made a terrible mistake.

CHAPTER SIX

GERMAIN EPISTLETHWAITE OPENED his eyes. Someone was banging at the front door, with what sounded to be a heavy fist in a metal glove. He was confused and his head felt thick and heavy, because it was the middle of the day and he never slept so late. The straw mattress, and the raggedy blanket that lay over him were damp with his sweat, and he felt exhausted despite the long rest.

There was a shuttered window in his room that opened up into the alleyway beside the workshop, and the light poked through it like sunlight through the trees. He could see the dust floating through the sunbeams and at any other time it would have felt peaceful and dreamy. But Germain knew this was no dream.

"The door, Barty!" he rasped, but as he said the words a fuzzy memory of Barthian saying goodbye flashed to the front of his mind. He called again, but there was no noise coming from the workshop where Barthian would normally be working away…just the insistent banging on the door.

"Hold on a moment!" Germain shouted, but his voice was as weak as his limbs. He could barely lift himself from the bed, let alone make his way to the door.

But the knocking had ceased, for the moment anyway. Perhaps the visitor had gone. Germain knew he wouldn't be so fortunate. He heard a scramble and a scrape, and the shuffling sound of a lot of people moving about in the street. There was the hiss of a fog boiler, the grinding of gears and the charging of an engine, following the spinning of wheels and trackers, and, finally, the almighty crash of metal upon wood as a Bombardier rushed the workshop door and smashed the whole thing to pieces, door frame and all.

The workshop and Germain's quarters filled with dust and clatter as pieces of wood and brick fell down upon the automaton, which just as aggressively reversed gear and backed away from its carnage. Germain wanted to shout, to leap out of bed and defend his home and his workshop, but it was no use. He hadn't the strength to do any of those things. He barely had the strength to turn his head and watch as a familiar, formidable figure stood in the doorway, profiled against the light streaming through the dust cloud.

"You have something that belongs to me," Overseer Grimm growled beneath a curling lip. "I've come to take it back. It's fixed, I hope."

Germain groaned and put his hand to his forehead, mumbling, "Barthian, where are you?"

Meanwhile, Grimm stepped inside, his boots crunching on the broken bits of doorway that lay at his feet. He glanced once around the workshop. "Where's the boy?" he demanded, approaching the bed and towering over Germain. Two Pacifier automatons followed Grimm into the room with their weapon arms extended, ready for trouble.

"If he's not in the workshop, then I don't know."

Grimm looked behind him at the door to the street, where a Troubleshooter waited for orders.

"Search the workshop for my watch!" Grimm barked. "Try not to break anything!"

"Aye, sir!" the automaton said, and went to work, searching for the watch and causing maximum damage while he went about it.

"Typical!" Grimm gave an exaggerated roll of his eyes as though dismayed by his automaton's work. "I can't take him anywhere!"

Timepieces of all description were knocked from shelves and sent crashing to the stone floor. All Germain could do was groan again as his entire livelihood, indeed his entire life's work, was destroyed by Grimm's minion.

"Please!" Germain managed to say, as despair and anger welled up inside him. "This is my son's future."

"Your son has no more of a future than you do," said Grimm.

When the automaton had finished its search, it stood behind Grimm and delivered the bad news.

"No sign of the watch, sir!"

Germain saw Grimm's hands clench into fists, and for a moment he expected Grimm to bring them both down upon his chest in a rage. But Grimm took a breath, straightened, and steadied himself. His voice was ice cold and murderous, spilling over with hatred and seething anger.

"Does the boy know who you are?" he asked.

Germain turned to look the Overseer in the eye. Now it was his turn to seethe with rage. "He knows what he needs to know!"

"So, he doesn't? He doesn't know what you did?"

Germain refused to speak.

Grimm walked to the foot of the bed and his exoskeleton hissed and huffed and blew jets of green fog as he moved. "I remember you, you know," he said. He looked away, as if concocting threats in his head and heart. "All those years ago, in the Great Engineer's court. You wouldn't remember me—how could you? I was just a guardsman, no more than an ornament fixed to the wall. But you...you were the promising apprentice, the special one, the one with the skills and the passion...but look at you now. Bedridden, crippled and weak. Poor. Alone. Abandoned. And look at me: everything that you will never be."

Germain turned away to avoid letting Grimm see his eyes, but it was too late - the tears were falling down his cheeks.

"Is it too much to hear?" Grimm asked, feigning concern. "Not so special now, eh, timekeeper? Not so gifted, now your master has fled. The Great Engineer, fleeing like a frightened child, leaving his loyal servants to fend for themselves."

From somewhere Germain found the strength to roll onto his side and raise himself on an elbow. He swung his legs out from under the woolen blanket and let his feet fall to the ground. He took a breath, then pushed with his hands on the straw mattress by his sides, determined to stand. But his determination was not enough to overcome his physical weakness, and he toppled backwards onto the bed, wheezing and cold.

Grimm hadn't finished. "You weren't so loyal though, as I remember." He walked around the bed and positioned himself in front of Germain, who was desperately trying to sit upright again. "Loyalty only at a price, eh timekeeper? The engineer must despise you for what you did."

"I was confused," Germain rasped. "I was tricked!"

"Tricked? I remember the Emperor rewarding you handsomely for your apparent loyalty."

"I denounced the Emperor. I still do."

"Of course you do," said Grimm, and clasped his robotic hand around the neck of the timekeeper. He grabbed a handful of Germain's shirt in his powerful metal fist and began to lift him from the bed by it.

The cloth tightened around Germain's already-struggling throat, sealing off his airways.

Grimm brought his face so close that Germain could feel the hot breath of the fog-powered villain. "The Emperor showed you mercy. But you! You—have—no—loyalty!"

Grimm threw him backwards and Germain gasped for air as he writhed on the bed in pain.

"Take him!" Grimm ordered the Pacifiers, who jumped to it and grabbed Germain beneath the arms, dragging him from the bed.

Germain hung limp as a rag doll in their arms, the last of his strength gone.

"I assume the boy has stolen the watch," Grimm said, clipped and official. "So, it's off to the Isle mines for you. If the boy returns the watch, I will let you go. If not, you will die in the mines, where you belong."

The automatons dragged Germain from the workshop, his boots scraping across the floor. As they passed out through the door of the workshop, he heard Grimm's voice behind him:

"You will rue the day you ever left the Fogworks," he shouted. "And so will your spawn!" Then to the Pacifier Officer standing outside in the street: "Get word out immediately. I want the boy caught and brought back to me...dead or alive!"

CHAPTER SEVEN

THE BIG PADDLE wheels of the old fog puffer turned endlessly as Amos Cleverley steered them further away from the fishing village, and further from the hooded man. The river sounds were hypnotic, from the gentle *slush*, *slush* of the paddles as they churned the water, to the gurgling of the four big fog boilers on the back of the boat, and the hissing sound of the exhausts as jet streams of green fog blew out the back. The river was wide enough for two boats about the same size as the fog puffer to pass one another easily, and on the banks the vegetation was green and lush—trees and shrubs, thick undergrowth and moss-covered rocks, and, beyond the banks, green and yellow fields, vast tracts of land covered in crops and grass.

"All this belongs to the Emperor now," Cleverley shouted from the back of the puffer, where he held the rudder and kept the boat away from the banks, where, he said, the river was shallow and the riverbed thick and muddy.

Cleverley's teeth were stained green, a sign that he chewed fog gum, which many of Aethasia's older folk did. Germain said the fog itself made them do it. After years of being exposed to the fog it became such a part of them that they craved it, more and more. Fog gum was a derivative of the fuel people used for their homes or to power their river boats, and it stained the teeth and discoloured the whites of their eyes. Germain had always warned Barthian to steer clear of people addicted to fog gum. But Cleverley was their only hope right now—and Lukas had vouched for him, after all.

"This land used to belong to the citizens of Aethasia," Cleverley continued. "All this food was shared among the people. Now all of it gets carted off to Evercity, where the Emperor and his cronies keep it for themselves. There hasn't been enough food to feed everyone…not since the Great Flood anyway."

Barthian frowned. "The Great Flood?"

"A huge amount of water flows off the mountain," Cleverley explained, indicating the snowy peaks of the Old Mount to their right. "These are some of the most fertile plains in the whole of Aethasia, but they were constantly under water. The Great Engineer built the pump houses along the river to drain the water and irrigate the fields, which turned this place into paradise."

Barthian could see one of the pump houses on the bank, and it was like nothing he had seen before—a tall, seven-sided building made from stone. Seven massive piston pumps, each with a great hinged arm, reached over from each side of the pump house into the water-logged ground around it.

"When the Great Engineer fled Evercity the pump houses fell into disuse and disrepair and the land was flooded by the waters from the mountain. For miles around, all you could see was water and the fields never fully recovered. Aethasia has been hungry ever since."

"Why didn't the Emperor just keep the pump houses going?" Nelly asked.

"Ah, my dear, you obviously haven't heard how much the Emperor despised the Great Engineer," Cleverley said. "In any case, he didn't have the expertise. There was a time when the usurper, back when he was the apprentice, was the brightest thing to come out of Evercity. But even he was nothing compared to the Great Engineer. He had a way with engines and pistons and pumps that the Emperor could never replicate."

"No one thinks of stealing the crops?" Salmon asked from inside the cabin.

Cleverley laughed, a big old meaty laugh from deep inside his belly.

"Don't think they haven't tried! They're in the Fogworks now, every last one of them!"

Barthian looked out through the small round window at the northern bank, through the trees and into the fields and their swaying, bright yellow crops. And yes, there was an automaton, and another, and another, patrolling the fields.

"Come here, lad," Cleverley said. "Take the helm for a while. Let's see if you'll make a puffer boat captain."

Barthian was happy to oblige. He leaned against the puffer's hull and took the rudder in his hand, then let the breeze hit him full in the face as he navigated the river. Nelly came and stood beside him, and grinned as the wind caught her hair and made her look more alive than Barthian had ever seen her.

"Wake me up when we're there!" Salmon called, stretching out on the bench beside the small table inside the cabin. He turned over with his face against the wall, the big hammer standing on the floor beside him.

"Tell me, lad," Cleverley said quietly to Barthian, as if he didn't want Nelly to hear. "Where are you off to, in such a hurry?"

"It's like Lukas said in the note," Barthian answered, annoyed at how little attention Cleverley seemed to have paid to the note's contents. "We need to go all the way to the Everbright Quay."

"That's an awful long way for a young boy and his urchin friends," Cleverley said. "What's out there that's so important? You know the Everbrights haven't lived in the old manor for thirty years?"

"I have no interest in the manor. I need to get to the Giant Seed Forest."

"The forest? Well, you're madder than I thought. There's no way into the forest, lad, not any more. And especially now the Emperor is building his new flagship there. The defenses...well, there's no way through, and the patrols have doubled along the highway."

"I'll find a way," Barthian said. "I have to."

"You know best," Cleverley said, with a chuckle. But right at that moment something scraped along the bottom of the hull of the puffer, and his chuckle stopped, abruptly.

"What was that?" Nelly asked in a high-pitched voice, her eyes wide.

"Oh, nothing!" Cleverley assured them, but the way his jaws shifted and his eyes darted about didn't seem to indicate that he thought it was nothing. "Just steer away from the bank a little more, lad. That's it. There are tree trunks and things of that nature stuck in the riverbed. Best we don't get snagged, not with your man in hot pursuit."

Barthian steered the puffer away from the northern bank and held its course in the centre of the river. It hardly mattered because there was no other river traffic. The River of Bones was deserted.

"Where are the other boats?" Barthian asked.

"What other boats?" said Cleverley. "People stay off the river these days. It's only crazy old coots like me who still make a living out of the trading posts."

"What's wrong with the river?"

"Yeah," Nelly added. "Why's it called the River of Bones?"

As she said it, there was another scraping sound along the bottom of the *Bitter Kiss*'s hull. Cleverley grabbed the rudder quickly and steered the boat even closer to the southern bank, before bringing the puffer back into the centre. He scanned the water intently, looking left over the port side, then straining his heavy neck so that he could see over to the right, the starboard side.

"What's—what's the matter?" Nelly asked. Her voice was quieter now, and Barthian thought he heard it shake.

Cleverley brushed her off. "Just the trees…and things."

"What things?" said Barthian.

"Just…things," Cleverley handed the rudder back to Barthian and headed inside the cabin, where they heard the sounds of him rummaging around for a minute or so. When he came back out there was a flintlock pistol shoved into his belt. He caught Barthian looking at it.

"Precautionary," he said. "Sometimes there are really big fish."

"I thought all the fish had died."

Cleverley said nothing, but he took the old rifle off the hull and held it in one arm, relaxed at his side.

But they continued without incident as the countryside rolled on by. The river began to veer inland and the peak of Old Mount, in the distant north, came into view. The trees on the banks became sparse, and the fields beyond lost both their colour and their crops. The land was scorched and empty, and covered with bracken like the moors. On the other bank, the land between the river and the sea was a wasteland of salt flats and dying trees, harsh vegetation and scavenging birds, circling for a feed. Barthian shuddered as he looked at it.

"It wasn't always like this," Cleverley said, seeing his reaction. "The days since the Usurping have been unkind to the land in these parts."

"The Usurping?"

"Aye, that's what some of us call it. But don't repeat the word off this boat. You'll be in big trouble."

"What was the Usurping?" Nelly said.

"The Usurping, lass, the day the Great Engineer fled Aethasia."

"I thought the Great Engineer was a myth," she said.

"Far from it," said Cleverley, chuckling again. "The place you're going, Everbright Manor, was the home of the Great Engineer."

Barthian had never heard this. His father didn't like to say too much about the Great Engineer, and certainly not about the end of his reign…and the beginning of the Emperor's rule.

"What happened on the day of the Usurping?" Barthian said.

"It was a terrible day for Aethasia, that's what happened." Cleverley looked genuinely sad as if the Usurping had happened only recently rather than thirty years ago. "The young master of the house, young Joshua Everbright, was murdered in the manor, while the Emperor and his cronies seized power for themselves."

"Murdered?" Nelly squeaked. "Who murdered him?"

"His own kin," said Cleverley. "His cousins, Jude and Magda. Filled with envy they were, with designs on the manor. The Emperor promised them the world, filled them with false dreams and wicked schemes… but for a great price. They had to deal with the young master."

Barthian stared at Cleverley. "They murdered their own blood relative?!"

"Well, everyone believes so. He hasn't been seen since that day. And all around, the land, the villages, the river settlements, have gone to waste and ruin. The young master never would have let that happen if he were still alive."

Cleverley went quiet, staring out at the river. Barthian went quiet too, suddenly far more daunted by this journey into the heart of that shadow, into the very darkness that dwelt over the Everbright Manor and the forest beyond.

The silence didn't last for long, however. The sound of more scraping against the hull shook them all from their reflections. But the sound wasn't the worst of it. Far more terrifying was the sight of an automaton climbing up the back of the boat and grabbing Nelly by the waist then pulling her down into the water, down into the River of Bones.

"*NELLY!*" Barthian screamed, so loud and long that it felt like fire in his throat.

"Hold on, boy!" said Cleverley, grabbing the rudder and manoeuvring the puffer towards the bank then back to where Nelly had been taken.

"What's happened?" Salmon asked, rushing from the cabin, his hammer in his hands.

"Nelly's in the water!" Barthian screamed. "Quickly! Do something!"

This was to Cleverley, not Salmon, but it was Salmon who responded first, diving immediately into the river and plunging into the darkness after Nelly.

"Salmon!" shouted Barthian, his voice going hoarse.

"Wait there, lad, wait!" Cleverley urged, bringing the puffer to a halt in the middle course of the river where the water was deepest.

But Barthian wasn't waiting, not at all. He threw himself into the river as well, kicking frantically with his feet and scrambling with his hands to get some equilibrium in the water, so that he could try and see what was going on. That's when he felt a hand on his leg.

Not a hand, actually, so much as a metal claw—the hand of an automaton, dragging him down into the swirling depths. Barthian heard a sudden crack, echoing and warped beneath the water, and saw a plume of bubbles streak past him from above. The automaton let go of his leg and sank away, incapacitated by the shot from Cleverley's rifle. Barthian scrambled upwards, fighting against the current pulling at his legs, so that he could at least break the surface and take a breath.

That's when he saw Salmon and Nelly, fighting against the water too, but also against an automaton, an old and mangled Trouble-shooter, clawing and flailing behind them. Barthian lunged forward and managed to grab the automaton around the neck. Spinning in the water he pulled it away from Nelly, who was suddenly yanked upwards out of danger by Cleverley, who flung her behind him into the cabin and aimed his rifle again.

"Wait, wait! You might hit Tick-Tock!" shouted Salmon, who suddenly lunged from the water like a great fish, and in a single motion brought the hammer up and over and crashing down upon the automaton's metal head. It fell away as well, giving Salmon and Barthian enough of a moment to scramble back to the puffer, where Cleverley pulled them aboard and dropped them like fish on the aft deck.

"It's not over!" Cleverley yelled, firing up the fog boilers so that the big paddle wheels started to turn.

"What are they?" shouted Salmon. "Where did they come from?"

"They're the rogue automatons, hunted by the Breakers all the way to the river, where they find can hide out in the water!"

Cleverley took the pistol from his belt. "Here they come!" he shouted, manoeuvring the puffer back around so that it was headed upriver once more. But in the time he had taken to turn the puffer mid-stream, automatons had clawed up the stern of the boat. "Quick lads, one of you stay with me, the other on the bow!"

Barthian ran along the gunwale between the cabin and the paddle wheels to the foredeck, where more automatons had climbed up the bow, and saw for the first time that they weren't complete. They had arms or legs missing, and some had lost their entire lower half. Their fog boilers were bubbling, but fog was spewing everywhere, from cracks and holes in the tanks and ruptures in the piping. He raised his gauntlet and hit the trigger.

Nothing. The automatons scrambled over the bow and onto the deck, so he fired again. Still nothing. He glanced quickly at the gauntlet, saw how wet it was, and realised the nodes weren't charging because they were cold and damp. The water all over him was shorting it out. He grabbed a rag from deck and swiped it across the gauntlet, just as a legless automaton crawled towards him—then pulled the trigger.

The arced lightning flashed from his arm and caught the crawling automaton on the helmet, knocking his head clean off. Then he fixed on another that was about to jump onto the deck and rush towards him with its one arm upraised. He blasted that one back into the water. Over on the port side of the foredeck another two automatons had helped one another over the bow and were raising themselves off the deck, ready to attack.

Barthian fired. One automaton blew apart, its limbs and boiler and helmet and torso flying in all different directions. He fired again and the remaining automaton was thrown from the boat.

Behind him, Salmon was busy too, but he was letting his hammer do the work. It was an impressive sight, watching Salmon swing the hammer up from below and catch an automaton on its chin, or swinging it above his head and seeing it come whizzing down upon an automaton's helmeted skull. Cleverley joined in, blasting an automaton that was trying to mount the boat over the port hull with his pistol.

And then they were done. The puffer was moving so fast that the automatons still scrambling at the hull were left behind in the water. Barthian joined Salmon and Cleverley on the aft deck, looking downriver at the wake from the puffer, and the churning white water where the automatons, stirred from their muddy graves, were still thrashing hopelessly about.

"What are they?" he asked again.

"The Emperor discards his damaged and irreparable automatons," said Cleverley. "Has done for years. Others turn mad and go AWOL. The Breakers chase them all over Aethasia and many of them ended up here. It's what killed the river trade. Most boats aren't fast enough to outrun them, and most skippers don't know the river well enough to avoid them. I haven't had trouble for a long time."

"Sorry," Barthian said.

"Nothing to do with you, lad. They saw an opportunity. Now you know why it's called the River of Bones. The lass isn't the first to be dragged into the river. She's one of the lucky ones."

They heard crying from inside the cabin, and Barthian realised all the fighting had made them forget about Nelly. He and Salmon went inside to where she crouched on the deck, beneath the table, dripping wet and shivering. Barthian put his arm around her shoulders and pulled her close.

"There are blankets down beside the chest," Cleverley shouted, carefully steering the puffer and watching for more trouble. "Get yourselves dry, or you'll be too sick to travel anywhere. We'll be at Lockeville soon and I'll make some soup."

"Give her something to eat," Salmon said, tossing a bag to Barthian. "I brought this."

Barthian looked into the bag and found bread, a potato, and a small bottle of syrup. "Here," he said. "Eat something. It will help with the shaking."

Nelly took the bread and tore off a mouthful. Barthian poured syrup over it and Nelly devoured it hungrily, though still shivering and unable to stop the tears. But the sweetness of the syrup soon soothed her nerves and her limbs stopped shaking. Barthian rubbed her arms to warm her up, as Salmon crouched beside them.

"This is just the beginning, Tick-Tock," he said, quietly. "We need to be ready for anything. There are darker things out there we haven't even imagined."

CHAPTER EIGHT

THE *BITTER KISS* sailed upriver throughout the afternoon, as Barthian, Salmon and Nelly huddled beside the little fogrock stove inside the cabin, wrapped in blankets while their clothes hung from a line that Cleverley had rigged across the foredeck from the metal limbs of a blasted automaton. The further they got from the scene of the attack, the more Nelly recovered from her shock and the less she shivered. The afternoon light changed the colours in the landscape, as the sun ahead of them began to fall across the distant forest and the Snowmoors beyond.

"We'll arrive at Lockeville before sundown," shouted Cleverley from the rudder. "I'll grab some supplies and make a nice barley broth. That'll fix you all."

"We're very lucky to have Amos along for the journey," Nelly whispered.

Salmon tossed a look at the big man's back. "I don't trust him."

"How can you say that?" Nelly protested. "He saved us from the hooded man, and he helped us fight off the automatons!"

"Yes, he did—but I still don't trust him."

"I don't think we have to trust him," Barthian said, "but we do need his help, at least for now. We'll reach Everbright Quay tomorrow, then it's on foot from there. As long as we keep our wits about us."

The afternoon wore on like the River of Bones and the rains eventually came, sweeping in from the ocean and spilling over the Riverlands. When the first rain fell, Barthian, Nelly, and Salmon brought in their clothes and warmed them by the fire, and by the time they were dressed the clothes were toasty, and it was the most like home they had been all day.

The rain clouds cleared and the sun was big and orange and hovered over the horizon by the time the puffer pulled up at the Lockeville landing. Barthian, Nelly, and Salmon were perched on the foredeck watching the banks sail by and the waters of the river peel away as the bow of the puffer pushed on and on. Lockeville came into view as they rounded a bend, and they were surprised to see actual people after almost a full day of seeing only Cleverley, the hooded man, and the rogue automatons.

Lockeville turned out to be no more than a big old white inn with a thatched roof, and barns and stables off to the side where travelers could rest and feed their horses. There were tables out front where men and women—mainly men—sat around drinking ale and eating bread with brisket gravy. From the boat, Barthian and the others could hear the men's laughter, but it was the sort of laughter they wanted to steer clear of—the scary laughter of people bigger and older and more worldly wise than them.

"Be a good lad," Cleverley said, throwing Salmon the rope. Salmon happily obliged, leaping off the puffer onto the bank and securing the rope around one of the bollards.

"We'll stay on the boat," Barthian said, ducking inside the cabin with Nelly.

"Suit yourself," Cleverley said, stepping up onto the bank with a huff and a wheeze. Even the slightest activity made him bright red in the face and neck. "You might be waiting a little while—I have business inside."

"I'll bet he does," said Salmon, as Cleverley stumped away towards the inn, where he was greeted with hearty welcomes from the men drinking ale at the tables outside, some of whom were looking curiously over to the puffer. Barthian felt uneasy at their stares, and moved quietly out of sight into the boat's small cabin, pulling Nelly with him.

Cleverley meant what he said about being a while. He was inside the inn for ages, and Barthian watched the sky turn orange and then pale and then grey and then eventually black. He began to pace the deck, worried that something unexpected had happened to the boatman. Every hour spent idle on the river was another hour that the hooded man would gain ground, if indeed he was still pursuing them. Cleverley had said they would eat supper, sleep for a while, then head off before the first light. But it was getting too late for all that.

"Should we head off on foot, Tick-Tock?" Salmon asked, sensing Barthian's impatience.

Barthian bit the inside of his cheek. "We're so far from home… but have so far to go."

"If we stick close to the road, we could make it to the manor by late morning."

Barthian gazed through the window at the inn and the raucous gathering that was continuing out the front. He saw no sign of Cleverley.

"I'm going to look for him," he said, suddenly.

"Don't do it!" Salmon said. "It will be dangerous in there."

"Exactly!" Barthian reasoned. "What if Cleverley's been waylaid? We could be here for days."

"I'm sure he'll be back soon," Nelly said, but Barthian could hear in the quietness of her voice that she was getting nervous as well.

As he pressed his nose against the small window, Barthian realised there was more to be concerned about than Cleverley being waylaid. One of the revelers on shore pointed towards him and shouted something at some of the others. Barthian had been spotted.

The man stood up, an ale in his hand, and began to stagger towards the riverbank. He was dressed like a wealthy merchant, with a big top hat and suit, and he was so unstable that he walked with a cane. One of his fellow revelers saw him stagger away and staggered after him, two of them now approaching the puffer.

"Get down!" Barthian shouted in a whisper.

Nelly did just that, but Salmon sprang to the window.

"What is it?"

"Two fellows, coming this way!"

"I'll grab the hammer."

"No Salmon, we can't fight. There's too many of them."

The men were at the boat, saying "Hello!" in slurring voices. The one in the top hat was trying to get aboard, though it took him longer than it should because he was so wobbly on his feet. The younger one didn't look like a merchant at all. He looked like a farm worker, and there was dirt on his hands and up the sides of his face, with bits of hay and sawdust in his hair and midges buzzing around his head.

"What have we here?" crowed the portly rich man.

"Well, well," stammered the younger one, who had terribly rotten teeth.

"I've a feeling you three might fetch a small fortune," added the first, stepping down into the cabin, the tankard of ale in one hand, the cane in the other.

But Salmon stood in his way, blocking his path with his hammer raised.

"My, my, that's no way to treat a perfectly decent stranger!" The man stepped back in artificial dismay as he said it, but the look in his eyes had hardened.

"No, but this is!" a voice growled from outside, and the large hands of Amos Cleverley saved them again, as he grabbed both men by the collars and slung them off the puffer. The merchant's tankard of ale went flying.

"You should know better Norval Hoggbin! Going about scaring my guests? What were you thinking?" Cleverley demanded. "And you! Silas Chickering!" Cleverley shouted at the younger one. "You're not fit to step aboard the *Bitter Kiss*, and you know it!"

Norval Hoggbin was flat on his backside on the bank, and Silas Chickering was leaning against him.

"But I…I only…you see I heard…" Hoggbin stammered.

"Not another word out of you," Cleverley shouted, giving Hoggbin a clout around the ear. "That's for your cheek. Any more and you'll get only my leftovers from this point on! Now, go on, beggar off! Off with you both!"

They slunk away, Hoggbin tottering against his walking cane and the younger man holding his other arm for support.

Cleverley came into the cabin with two sacks. He placed both on the floor, and Barthian noticed that one of them sagged as though heavy with supplies, but the other, although full and bulging, seemed much lighter weight.

"Cast off, would you!" Cleverley barked at Salmon. "And stay on the bank until we're through the lock!"

"Cast off?" Barthian asked. "But it's dark. You said we would eat, and stay here for the night."

"I've changed my mind. We're heading upriver where it's safe and away from prying eyes. Then we'll have supper."

Salmon cast off and stayed on the bank as Cleverley had told him, to unlock the first set of giant paddles with the windlass. Barthian watched through the window as Salmon cranked the lock key, round and around. The *Bitter Kiss* edged forward and sat between the first and second paddles as the water rushed from beneath them and dropped the puffer to the River of Bones' lower level. Beyond Salmon, over near the inn, Hoggbin and his young friend were stirring up conversation, gesturing back towards the boat in a heated way. A small gang formed and started to wander over.

"Be fast about it!" shouted Cleverley as Salmon worked the last paddles. Finally, the *Bitter Kiss* was moving from the lock. "Leave the gates!" Cleverly shouted. "Get back aboard!"

Salmon jumped aboard as the inn crowd ran towards the bank, hollering and waving their arms. He joined Barthian and Nelly down below.

"What was that all about?" he asked, breathing heavily.

"I don't know," Barthian said. "But I don't like it."

"Me neither," said Nelly, gripping both their hands.

Cleverley fired up some fog lamps on the front of the puffer, and they lit up the river with a ghostly green mist. Then Cleverley cranked up the boilers some more, and the paddle wheels churned.

Away they went, back onto the river's middle course to continue their voyage as Cleverley remained at the rudder as before, except deep in thought and more quiet than he had been all day.

Barthian didn't have the heart to ask him what was wrong, but he knew that something had happened at Lockeville to change Cleverley for the worse.

⁓

Whatever was wrong with Cleverley, it didn't stop him keeping to his word and cooking up a nice, big stew once they were well clear of Lockeville. With Salmon at the helm, steering the puffer slowly and steadily upriver in the near pitch black darkness, Cleverley joined Barthian and Nelly in the cabin and chopped up the vegetables he'd fetched from the inn, throwing them in a big pot with a handful of barley and a handful of some kind of strange-smelling seasoning. Then he took the rudder again while the stew cooked, and followed the fog lamps on the bow into the darkness as the night stretched on. In time, the aroma from the stew filled the cabin, an intoxicating and mesmerizing whiff of home-cooked goodness. The children from No Man's Landing had rarely experienced such smells, and now it made their noses twitch and their mouths water.

"I'm starving!" Nelly whispered to Barthian, who chuckled.

"Not long to wait now."

"It smells like magic."

"I suppose it does."

"I didn't see him drop any meat in there," said Salmon, disappointed. "Not even a fish. A bit of beef would have been perfect, but a mackerel or two would have been all right."

"It'll be delicious, I'm sure," said Barthian, who fancied a bit of beef himself.

The stew wasn't delicious—not at all. The vegetables weren't even cooked through. But they didn't complain, because all three of them were starving and would have been happy with Barthian's raw potato. They ate together at the table, with Cleverley perched on a crate, slurping up the stew like he hadn't eaten in a week. He was loud and sloppy, and the watery soup spilled over his chin and down his neck.

Nelly never said a word the whole time—she was too caught up gnawing at the firm carrots that she spooned straight from the pot, which she shared with Barthian and Salmon while Cleverley ate from the only bowl on the boat. Salmon ate grumpily, but Barthian could tell by the way he wiped his mouth and kept going to the pot for more that he hadn't eaten this well for a while.

After supper, Cleverley fired up the puffer again as the others cleaned up. They made good distance and passed the old settlement of Mill Stone, which Salmon said was haunted and was one place he wouldn't like to be stranded at night.

"What do you mean, haunted?" Nelly asked, watching through the window as the abandoned old mill loomed high above the trees, black and hulking, its bulk blocking out the dim starlight of the night sky.

"People go missing in Mill Stone," Salmon said.

"Missing?"

"Yeah, missing. There are ghosts in that old mill. Ghosts of automatons!"

"Automatons don't have ghosts," Barthian said, trying to quell Nelly's fear.

"These ones do!" Salmon said, and wouldn't be told otherwise.

They bedded down for the night on the floor of the cabin while the puffer continued upriver and images of automaton ghosts assailed their thoughts. It wasn't the best way to prepare for sleep, but they were exhausted from the day's travels, so weary that not even scary stories about make-believe automaton ghouls would keep them awake.

"No harm in making the most of the darkness and getting further upriver," Cleverley called out to them as they settled down. "I'll have you at Everbright Quay by first light at this rate."

And so Barthian nodded off, contented by the amount of food in his belly, and finally relaxed about the distance they were putting between the boat and the hooded man...and Lockeville...and the rogue automatons living on the riverbed. He still had a concern or two about Cleverley, but at the end of the day they were headed in the right direction, and they had showed Cleverley during the battle with the automatons that they knew how to take care of themselves in a tussle. Barthian couldn't foresee any danger between here and the Quay, so he closed his eyes and let sleep take him, secure in the thought that the morning would bring the end of their trip upriver. And then it was onto the final stage of their journey.

But Barthian woke well before the morning came.

What's more, he woke in confusion, with his hands tied, and a gag in his mouth making it hard to breathe. He opened his eyes but saw only darkness—not just because it was the middle of the night, but because he was inside one of the sacks Cleverley had brought aboard from the inn.

"Gerrrrooooooofff!" Barthian shouted. He tried to kick his way out of the sack with his legs but they were tied at the ankles as well. "Grrrrrrrrrhhh!"

"Steady on, young Barthian," he heard Cleverley say, and the big man placed his hand on Barthian's head and pressed him to the floor. "There's no way out of that sack. I've tied you up good and proper."

That didn't stop Barthian. He thrashed and buckled and writhed and punched, but it was just as Cleverley had said—there was no way out of the sack. Barthian began to panic, just like in the tunnel to the Pool of Stars. He hated small spaces, now here he was, in a sack, tied up like an animal, with a rag fastened around his head and gagging his mouth. He thrashed again, but Cleverley pushed him flat to the floor of the cabin, and with more force.

"I wouldn't struggle so much if I were you!" Cleverley said, in a coldly menacing way. "I'll drop your little girlie friend in the river if you don't stop."

Barthian did as he was told, despite how much he wanted to kick and scream. The last thing he wanted was any more misfortune happening to his friends. He felt for the gauntlet on his wrist, hoping he might blast his way out of the sack. But the gauntlet was gone.

"Nnnlly!" he tried to say.

"Nghhh!"

Nelly was there, beside him on the cabin floor, probably tied up and secured in a sack as well.

"Sssmon!"

"Yyyp!"

Salmon was there too, and gagged like the others.

"That's enough. Quiet!" Cleverley barked. "You're feeling groggy because I put a little something in your stew. But you're all here, and you're all safe … for now. You're worth more to me alive than dead. But that doesn't mean I won't drop you all in the river if you give me too much trouble."

"Whhy?" Barthian shouted.

"Why? Because there's a price on your heads, that's why. It appears the hooded man isn't the only one on your tail. Grimm wants you back in No Man's Landing, and he's willing to pay for it. What can I say? I need the coin."

Barthian heard Cleverley push himself up from the floor where he had finished tying the sacks.

"I'll be turning the boat around and taking you back to Heron's Rush," Cleverley growled. "I sent word from Lockeville last night that I'll have you there in the morning. You'll be met by an automaton patrol and taken back to No Man's Landing."

"Nnnno!" Barthian shouted again, and would have thrashed some more, except he didn't want Nelly to be dropped in the river. But uppermost in his mind was his sick father, and the Aether Rose, and the tonic Lukas wouldn't be able to make without it. The thought of Lukas made Barthian even more confused. How could Lukas have gotten it so wrong by sending him to a scoundrel such as Cleverley. "Luuuas!" Barthian shouted.

"Quieten down," Cleverley called back. He was firing up the fog boilers ready to crank up the big paddle wheels.

"Luuuas!" Barthian shouted again.

"I can't understand a word you're saying, boy! Pipe down!"

"Luuuas!" Barthian persisted. He was desperate to remind Cleverley of his obligation to his supposed friend.

"Ohhh, Lukas?" Cleverley said, finally clicking. "You're saying Lukas! You think I should let you go, because of Lukas, my old friend!"

"Ysss!" Barthian said, nodding, even if Cleverley couldn't see his head through the sack. "Luuuas!"

"I take your point!" said Cleverley. "Thing is…I'm not Cleverley. Never have been. Cleverley's long gone—hasn't been seen around these parts since I won the *Bitter Kiss* in a game of chance at the end of a long night of ale and cards and fog gum at the Lockeville inn! I brought you along for the ride because I hoped there'd be some coin in it…and here we are. Turns out it was a good investment!"

Barthian groaned, and he could hear Nelly and Salmon groaning too. They had heard every word, and knew the implications. They were headed back to the village to be handed over to Grimm's automatons, and there was nothing they could appeal to in order to change Cleverley's mind (or whatever his name was).

The boilers powered up the puffer's engines, and the engines turned the paddle wheels. Barthian felt the boat pull away from its mooring and head upriver, in the direction of Everbright Quay, and for the quickest moment he wondered whether 'Cleverley' had actually changed his mind. But no, no such fortune. The puffer began to turn in mid-river as the dark waters slushed around them, and then it was off again, travelling downriver at speed, towards Grimm and his waiting automatons…in the opposite direction entirely from the Everbright Quay, the Giant Seed Forest, and the rare Aether Rose.

CHAPTER NINE

DEEP BENEATH THE Isle off the coast from No Man's Landing, the mines tunneled down into the earth as the Emperor's Minion automatons burrowed away at the veins of fogrock that kept Aethasia powered up and beaten down. Enemies of the Emperor worked alongside the automatons, shoveling up their rock and dumping it in hoppers, which were then carted through the mines on miles and miles of rail track, all the way back to the surface where huge cranes dumped the rock into a mine bulker that sailed back and forth to the docks in No Man's Landing, every day, and every night.

It was dark and dusty and hot as a furnace in the deepest tunnels where the richest deposits of fogrock glistened like fake jewels in the bedrock. It was no place for Aethasians, but under the Emperor's rule the unfortunate ones slaved over their tools from the moment they woke to the moment they slept, guarded by armoured automatons and commanded by cruel Autofficers, all of whom answered to one man: Overseer Grimm.

Grimm lorded over the mines and the mine workers like the Emperor lorded over Aethasia. Out of sight and mind from the court in Evercity, Grimm treated the Isle like his own kingdom, driving his automated and human slaves to produce more and more fogrock, which in turn curried more and more favour with the Emperor. He needed the rock to build his armies, and to construct and power his airships, and he rationed just enough to the inhabitants of Aethasia that they remained dependent on the Emperor for their very lives… and grateful for it.

Grimm rarely descended to the lower levels, but he made an exception for Germain Epistlethwaite, who he had ordered to the very darkest section of the mines.

"I hope you're enjoying the view," Grimm said, as Germain stood before him, flanked by Pacifier Officers.

"It's very refreshing," Germain answered defiantly.

"It will do wonders to your lungs!" Grimm said, with a sneer. "I'm told the air down here is quite lovely in the heat of the day."

"The sun is overrated," Germain said. "Give me a nice, dark tunnel any day."

"Well, soak it up. There'll be no time for mending watches here."

"Good thing you don't have one to mend."

Grimm went silent for a moment, and Germain could imagine his eyes glaring from behind his green fogged-up lenses.

"You will die here," Grimm said with glee. "When you do, I'll command that they leave your body where it drops, hidden in some dark and lonely tunnel, where your boy will never find you. He will live out his days wondering what happened to his 'father'…but no one in all of Aethasia will be able to tell him."

It was Germain's turn to be silent. Grimm turned and walked away, joined by his Officers. Germain gave him one final message.

"You underestimate my boy at your peril," he said. "He is the true timekeeper, more gifted than I ever was. He would have made a fine apprentice to the Great Engineer."

"A pity then, that we will never know…since the Great Engineer is dead."

"Dead he may be…but who knows?"

Grimm paused, and Germain continued:

"Who do you think is behind the slowing of Aethasia's clocks? The Emperor? He didn't invent clockwork, the Great Engineer did. Your time is running out, Grimm. The countdown has begun."

Grimm stood with his back turned to Germain, who had propped himself up against his shovel handle to stand as straight and tall as he could—despite feeling like he was about to collapse. He steadied himself for a response, perhaps a swift strike with Grimm's metallic hand or a blow from one of the Officers. But it never came. Grimm walked away into the darkness of the tunnels, leaving Germain alone in the depths, surrounded by the noise of constant drilling and the thick cloud of fog dust.

Germain knew these tunnels well; being thrown into the mines and left to rot was the price he had paid for initially supporting and then renouncing the newly-coronated Emperor. But when the mines didn't break Germain, he got thrown into the Fogworks instead, where life was even more terrible for the Emperor's enemies than in the mines.

But not even the Fogworks could break the spirit of Germain Epistlethwaite, who proved as clever at finding ways out of a prison as he was with clockwork mechanics. But that was many years ago when he was a much younger man, before the green lung made him old and weak ahead of time. Now, even the thought of tunneling out of the Fogworks or the Isle or wherever else the Emperor tried to hold him, made him wheeze and cough.

So, there he stood, in the bowels of the fogrock mine, assigned to a squad of Minions that were burrowing their drilling snouts deep into the rock, as deadly green dust mixed with the fog from their boilers and polluted the tunnel. Behind him stood a Pacifier, tall and sturdy, its weapon raised to attention, watching Germain's every move.

"Work!" the Pacifier commanded, and took a step closer. If Germain wasn't careful, the Pacifier would jab at him with its bayonet again—except this time, as well as tearing his boiler suit, it might just as easily pierce his skin. That would be curtains.

Germain got back to work, as the grimy sweat laced his body and his underclothes stuck to his skin. It wasn't that he was afraid of the Pacifier—he had noticed that the one Grimm had assigned to him was a rusty, long-out-of-date model—and he certainly wasn't afraid of hard work. He wasn't even afraid of dying, and had reconciled in his mind that no matter how successful Barthian was at finding an Aether Rose, he did not have long to live. That didn't bother him.

What bothered him was the thought of never seeing Barthian again; of never being able to tell him the truth about his past; of missing out on the chance to set him on a good course for the future. That terrified him, and he was determined to let no one—not the Pacifier, not Grimm, not even the Emperor himself—get in the way of that.

So, he scooped up the loose fogrock with his big, wide shovel, and threw it into the hopper sitting on the tracks beside him. Then he did it again, and again. He shoveled until his back ached, until his lungs felt as heavy as freshly-filled water skins. Then he turned and walked to the Pacifier, which quickly said 'Halt!' before Germain smacked it sideways with the big shovel. The automaton tried to fire at him but one of its rusty joints locked, throwing it off balance, and it toppled over. Germain stepped around it, and continued on to the containment room in a cleft of the mine across from the Minions' dig site.

The containment room was sparse, save for some old Minion spare parts, a couple of replacement driller snouts, and a decommissioned Techno Mite—the small utility and repair bots that accompanied every mining squad and automaton patrol. He wasn't looking for any of those though—he was looking for the chest that held the dynamite, used for breaking up the rocky underground bulkheads.

The chest was locked, of course, but Germain was the Timekeeper—what was a little lock to an expert in clockwork? He found the dynamite and a lighter and was lighting the fuse on a single stick of dynamite as he walked back out into the tunnel, just as the Pacifier was getting back up off its feet.

"Pacify this!" Germain said, slotting the dynamite into the heavy grille that covered the small furnace inside the automaton's chest. As the automaton became flustered, wondering what in Aethasia that fuse was doing sparking away in its torso, Germain hurried back inside the containment room, where he waited until the blast flung the Pacifier in a hundred different pieces across the tunnel.

Germain grabbed and lit two more sticks as an urgent sound echoed off the walls of the tunnel. Minions had heard the blast and were rushing to see what the commotion was all about.

"A little something to clear your snouts!" Germain wanted to shout it, but breathing was too difficult, so he contented himself with just thinking it. He tossed the sticks of dynamite over to where the Minions were standing, bewildered, their drilling cones still spinning and flicking off fog dust and bits of green rock.

They had no time to move. The dynamite blasted the Minions and the rock face behind them, bringing a section tumbling down and burying them beneath a pile of granite and fogrock. Germain could hear the blast echoing away up the tunnels and throughout the mine, and listened for a moment to see whether the explosion had caused a chain reaction. The rock down here was very stable and solid, so any damage should have been contained to his section of the mine—the prisoners in the other areas should still be perfectly safe.

When he was satisfied the structural integrity of the mine system hadn't been compromised, Germain hopped aboard the hopper, reached over and yanked the lever, then found himself trundling through the tunnels as the hopper joined the main tracks and fell in with a hundred other carts that were making their way to the surface of the Isle... and freedom.

CHAPTER TEN

BARTHIAN FELT MOVEMENT beside him on the floor of the cabin, followed by the sound of sackcloth being ever-so-quietly cut open. He held his breath because the sound of air entering and exiting his nostrils was making it too difficult to hear what was going on beside him, so he lay there dead still, his ear poised in the direction of the sound.

Then a hand touched his arm, someone whispered "Shhh!" and the blade of a long knife entered his sack near his waist. It cut a long slither all the way to his head, so that finally he could see again…and there were Salmon's big, brown eyes, peering through a similar opening in his own sack, and looking right back at Barthian. Salmon held the knife that he'd fastened to his leg before they left No Man's Landing, which Barthian had completely forgotten about. Thankfully, "Cleverley" had never laid eyes on it, or he would have taken it along with the gauntlets and Salmon's big hammer.

Salmon held a finger to his lips. "Shhh!" he whispered again, but Barthian had no intention of making any sound. Salmon reached through the opening he had made with the knife, and cut the rags binding Barthian's hands. Then he gave Barthian the knife so that he could cut the rags from around his ankles.

"OY!" came a shout from the back of the puffer, where Cleverley was still steering the boat downriver. The big man rushed from the rudder, letting the puffer steer itself, and thundered into the cabin where he could see his prisoners trying to escape. But Salmon and Barthian were too quick. Salmon sprung from his sack first and leapt into the path of the oncoming kidnapper, whose face was purple with rage.

Salmon was bigger than Barthian, but even so he was no match for Cleverley, who grabbed him by the shoulders and threw him against the cabin wall beside the fog burner. But Barthian was up on his feet already, and Barthian had the knife. He held it up towards the fat man's wobbly belly, even though actually using it was the last thing he intended to do.

Cleverley must have seen the fear in his eyes and known that Barthian would never intentionally hurt anyone. He lunged forward, grabbing Barthian by the wrist and flinging the knife from his hand. Then he shoved Barthian, who stumbled over backwards, tripping over the sack that still held Nelly on the floor of the cabin. As Barthian fell he saw Salmon take another leap, pushing off the wall and springing towards Cleverley like a wild animal, flailing with his fists and howling out loud.

"Yaaaarrr!"

Salmon landed full in the boatman's chest, knocking him backwards against the starboard side of the cabin. It was as much his own weight that made Cleverley fall, the huge girth around his belly making him lopsided and unsteady.

"The hammer!" shouted Salmon, pointing at the weapon on the table where their captor had left it. Salmon's catapult gauntlet and Barthian's weapon were there too, but it was the hammer that Barthian grabbed and tossed to Salmon before Cleverley could stand up again.

Salmon raised the hammer high, as if he would have gladly brought it down on the big man's belly.

"Nooo!" shouted Barthian, and Salmon stayed his hand, glaring at Cleverley and threatening to strike.

"He's had us tied up in sacks, like rats!" Salmon shouted. "You tell me why I shouldn't wallop him?"

"Because that makes you as bad as he is!" Barthian said.

"He needs a taste of his own medicine," Salmon insisted, still with the hammer raised.

"Maybe so," said Barthian. "But not from us."

There was a groan from the floor, where Nelly was kicking and writhing to get their attention.

"All right, Nelly!" Barthian called to calm her down. "Salmon, let's stop the boat and get off. He can't do anything to us now."

It wasn't Cleverley they needed to worry about, though, it was the *Bitter Kiss* itself. Without Cleverley at the helm, the puffer had charged ahead into the darkness and was running at full engine-power towards a bend in the river, with the bank fast approaching. It crashed into the trees as the hull hit the muddy riverbed, tearing a hole in the boat's side as it hit tree trunks and goodness knows what else.

Everyone inside the cabin went flying, except Nelly, who rolled around the floor in her sack. By the time Barthian and Salmon had come to their senses, Cleverley had Salmon's hammer, and was holding it high above them, preparing to strike.

"Not so tough now, eh HORRO!"

"Oy, that's insulting!" said Salmon, at the fat man's use of the offensive term for the Horizon People.

Behind Cleverley, an automaton had lifted itself up from the riverbed into the stricken puffer and was climbing over the stern, between the two pairs of fog boilers.

"Look!" Barthian pointed. "Automatons!"

"Nice try!" said Cleverley.

The closest automaton's hand made a metallic scraping noise along the edge of the hull, and Cleverley's eyes widened as he realized it wasn't a ruse.

He turned and charged at it with the hammer, knocking it back into the black depths from which it had hoisted itself. Barthian saw his chance. He grabbed the leather gauntlet from the cabin floor and slipped it back onto his wrist. As the boatman jumped back down into the cabin to finish them all off, Barthian raised the gauntlet and leveled it squarely at his chest.

"I won't hesitate…and I won't miss." He gulped and tried to keep his hands from visibly shaking as he said it.

"You don't have the nerve!" Cleverley sneered.

"I didn't, you're right," Barthian admitted. "But then you threatened my friends."

Cleverley must have been convinced, because he didn't make another move.

Barthian held him there until Salmon had freed Nelly, collected his hunting gauntlet and his knife, and taken the hammer from the boatman. Then Barthian grabbed his sack and the three of them climbed from the puffer onto the bank, scrambling through the branches of the trees until they were on firm ground. Meanwhile, Cleverley fired up his fog boilers again, and began to reverse the stricken boat away from the bank.

"There's a great hole in the hull!" Barthian shouted to the boatman. "You'll sink in the river!"

"Leave him!" said Salmon. "The fat old fool deserves what he gets!"

"We can't just let him drown," Barthian said.

"If he wants to stick with a sinking boat that's his problem!"

"Let him go!" said Nelly, who was tired of the whole dark episode. "Let's just get far away from the river and the monsters."

But Barthian shouted again. "Cleverley! Whatever your name is! The boat will sink!"

As it pulled away from the bank, the old puffer began to list as it took on water. This wasn't the boatman's biggest problem, though. As it listed, the automatons returned, scrambling up the side of the boat.

The children heard Cleverley shouting, saw the flash of a rifle shot, and a jumble of movement as the automatons overwhelmed him.

Cleverley was never going to win a battle like that alone, and no one deserved to die that way. So Barthian responded in the way that came naturally: he scrambled back through the trees and leapt onto the puffer from a thick branch that extended out over the water.

"Barty!" Nelly screamed.

"You fool, Tick-Tock!" shouted Salmon.

But Barthian had Lukas's gauntlet and he'd proven already that he knew how to use it. He blasted one, two, three automatons off the boat, then rushed to the rudder where Cleverley was being overwhelmed.

"Come on!" he called to the big man, pulling at his arm. "It's your last chance!"

"Let go of me you little aetherflake!" Cleverley shouted, pushing Barthian away. But Barthian wasn't giving up yet.

"Come with me NOW!" he screamed, blasting one automaton on the port side, and another on the starboard gunwale. He grabbed Cleverley by the belt and tried to yank him from his place beside the rudder. But Cleverley was twice as heavy as Barthian and he wouldn't budge. He pushed the boy away again.

"Tick-Tock!" Salmon shouted from the bank. "Time's running out!"

Barthian reluctantly turned and saw that the half-submerged puffer was now moving quickly away from the bank. Salmon was right. It was his last chance. He jumped to the gunwale beside the cabin, which was now the part of the boat that stood tallest from the water, and leapt into the bushes on the riverbank, scrambling with his hands among the branches. He felt his feet fall in the river water and the slick, slimy mud of the bank gave way underneath him, dragging him deeper into the water with nothing to get a foothold on.

But he hadn't reckoned on the quick-thinking of Nelly and Salmon, who had plunged into the trees and were pulling him ashore by the wrists. On the riverbank at last, and free from the sinking puffer and the dark swirling waters, Barthian turned with his friends and watched as the *Bitter Kiss* floated away, barely above the water now as the automatons swept in from all sides and devoured the boat and everything in it, like Snowmoorian scorpions. And then it was gone.

Salmon stared after the sinking boat for a moment, then shrugged. "I told you he'd get what he deserved."

"It's horrible!" said Nelly. Barthian wasn't sure whether she was referring to Cleverley's death or Salmon's reaction to it—or both.

Barthian's shoulders drooped. "I tried. He didn't want to be saved." He resented their captor as much as the others, but that didn't mean Cleverley couldn't have been turned around.

"We didn't even know his name," Nelly said.

"And now Grimm's watch is lost forever!" Salmon flung his arms in the air in frustration.

"You're wrong about that," said Barthian, holding out his hand and showing them the watch, sitting in the centre of his palm.

Salmon's eyes popped as big as saucers. "How—when—how?!"

"I took it from his pocket when I was trying to pull him off the boat," Barthian said. "It wasn't his to take to the bottom of the river."

He held the watch tightly in his hand as they turned from the riverbank and found the forest road, then they walked forward together into the night, on towards their journey's end.

⁂

"I know where we are!" Salmon exclaimed.

They had walked for the best part of an hour, with no indication of how far from Everbright Quay they were, nor how far downriver Cleverley had taken them while they were tied up in the sacks. It was the darkest part of night, and now that Barthian had Grimm's watch back in his possession they could at least keep track of the time. But above them, the night sky was darkening as storm clouds gathered. A big downpour was on its way and they needed shelter, and somewhere to rest. Their steps had gotten gradually slower and heavier as the miles went by, and they would need rest before they pushed on to the final leg of their journey. Barthian was afraid that if they didn't rest soon, he'd just fall down sound asleep on the spot.

"Where's that then?" Nelly asked Salmon, looking around for signposts or landmarks, anything that would tell them where they were.

"We're approaching Mill Stone!"

"Mill Stone?" Barthian said. "You said it was haunted."

"So the stories say."

"Shouldn't we go around then, and give it a miss?" Nelly asked. "I've never been anywhere haunted before, and I don't especially want to now."

"Oh, it's—it's not really haunted," Salmon said, despite how insistent he had been about it earlier. "They make up the stories because the place is abandoned."

"It sounds haunted to me," Nelly said.

"There's a big old mill, that's all," Salmon said, shrugging. "It's perfect shelter. We'll be able to camp there until first light."

Salmon was right about needing shelter. When the rain began, it fell heavily, as though a bucket was being poured from the sky. The lightning flashed as well, and lit up the road ahead of them.

"The mill! Did you see it!" Salmon asked, running ahead.

"Yes!" Barthian shouted. "But are you sure?"

"Come on!" Salmon called, without hesitating. The rain was falling so heavily that Barthian and Nelly could barely see Salmon as he bolted forward and was lost in the downpour. Barthian grabbed Nelly's hand and helped her along, because her boots were sloshing around in the mud and almost flying from her feet. The lightning flashed again and they could see just for a fleeting moment that the mill was closer, looming high above them into the clouds off the road to the left. They caught a glimpse of Salmon too, running through the bushes around to the riverside of the mill, where its big, static waterwheel sat in a channel off the main waterway.

"Wait for us!" Nelly shouted, but the sound of her voice was muffled by the rain.

"He can't hear you!" Barthian said, grabbing her hand. "Come on!"

They followed Salmon around to where the big old barn doors of the mill were hanging off their bolts, and they scrambled inside. Salmon was already there, shaking the rain from his matted hair like a wet dog, a lighter in his hand making his face glow.

"See!" he said, smiling. "Not haunted at all!"

"What is this place?" Barthian asked.

"It's Mill Stone," said Salmon, "the tallest building in the whole of Aethasia. Or it used to be. The Emperor built it when he was just an apprentice, before the Great Engineer left Evercity. He wanted to show off what a great designer and builder he was. He brought workers from all over Aethasia to build it, including some of my Horizon People, even people from Nautilina. He was showing off. It was so tall no one could see the top, taller than anything anyone had ever seen…until the top of it collapsed and killed a bunch of the mill workers. It's been deserted ever since."

"What happened to all the people who came from all over the world?" Nelly asked.

"Oh, they scarpered," said Salmon. "Back to where they came from."

Barthian stared at Salmon in awe. "How do you know these things?" he asked.

"The grotto is full of characters who love to tell stories," Salmon said. "What else do they have to keep themselves entertained?"

"It's true," said Nelly. "They sit around the fire and share stories of the old days, back before they lost everything."

Barthian looked around the dark interior, his mind struggling against the ghost stories Salmon had told earlier. Above them, rain roared on the roof, and Barthian tried to convince himself that the sounds lower down, all around them, were just raindrops falling through leaks in the roof onto the floor.

It was dark inside the ground floor but when lightning flashed outside a set of tall windows Barthian could just see an iron staircase up to the next level.

"Let's check out upstairs," he said, "away from the doors, just in case."

"In case what?" Nelly asked.

"Yeah, in case what?" Salmon echoed.

"I don't know—anything!" Barthian said, but he was thinking of the hooded man. They had wasted a lot of time trying to get free from Cleverley and the *Bitter Kiss*, and there was every reason to believe the hooded man was still on the hunt.

They headed cautiously to the back of the millhouse, listening for sounds of ghosts, and trod quietly up the iron staircase. The old mill had long been abandoned, as Salmon had said, but some of the old machinery had been left, such as a huge fog-powered shredder and a big round vacuum pan. Crates were still stacked against the back wall and a few barrels were left here and there, not to mention old fog boilers and fog burners and a big old fogrock pit.

The second floor was much the same, except there was no machinery, just crates and barrels stacked randomly in the darkness. There were storerooms around the exterior wall, and great steel girders that ran from ceiling to floor, part of the old mill's iron framework. The storm outside was heavier now and the noise of the rain and the wind, and the flashes of lightning and roars of thunder swept through the open window spaces in each of the darkened storerooms, sending a ghoulish sound throughout the mill.

"That's why they say it's haunted, I'll bet," said Salmon, and for once Barthian was inclined to agree with him.

"What about those noises—do you keep hearing them?" she asked.

"Of course we do, Chops!" said Salmon. "It's called a gale!"

"No, not the storm. Other noises."

Barthian stopped and listened. There was nothing. At least, nothing that he could hear.

"I don't hear anything," Salmon said. "Let's break up one of those barrels and start a fire. I reckon we sleep here for a few hours, and set off for the manor just after first light."

"Sounds good to me," Barthian said. "Nelly?"

"You don't hear it?" she asked again.

All Barthian could hear, apart from the storm battering the old mill, was the sound of his own yawning. He was desperate to sleep. He couldn't bear the thought of walking for another half day without giving his weary limbs a rest. He loved the idea of a fire, and stretching out on a firm floor, like home.

They broke up an empty barrel using Salmon's hammer and were able to scoop up enough bits of old chaff to get a fire going in no time, using Barthian's flint. They piled it high, but not too high, because Barthian was wary about the hooded man and didn't want to risk drawing his attention to the sight of orange firelight burning inside the supposedly abandoned mill. But even that care was cast aside as they sat together round the fire and warmed their hands against the flames. It was the best they had felt for many hours, and it wasn't long before they were all yawning like Barthian.

"That's me done," said Salmon, stretching.

"Me too!" Barthian moaned, already feeling his eyes close.

"Yep, me too!" said Nelly.

"Me too!" said a strange, mechanised fourth voice.

Everyone turned to look towards the voice, and Nelly screamed a blood-chilling scream that was louder than any storm. Sitting beside her was an automaton—not like the ones they were used to from No Man's Landing, the Pacifiers and Troubleshooters—it was the size of a small child, and looked almost…human. It had arms and legs, a round, steel-plated head, and glowing purple eyes.

There were no weapons attached to it that they could see, and in its chest was an exposed animus servo, a complex clockwork-driven device of multiple cogs and an actual clock face that replicated the human heart. Barthian had heard about them from Germain but had never laid eyes on one himself. The creature was an automaton, no doubt about it, but it was like nothing any of them had ever seen before.

Salmon was up on his feet and had the hammer in his hands as quick as the flashes of lightning still striking outside. But then something grabbed his wrist from behind and wrenched the hammer from his grip. It was another automaton, just like the first, but with different facial features.

"No, no, no!" it said, shaking its head.

Then from all around them, emerging from the shadows, came an avalanche of mechanised voices echoing the first: "No, no, no!"

More automatons stepped forward towards the fire.

"No, no, no!" they repeated, and the refrain got louder as more automatons crept out of the darkness and encircled Barthian, Salmon and Nelly. There were maybe ten, then twenty, then as many as fifty automatons, all of them like small children, each one with different facial features and apparently unique mannerisms, and each with an animus servo in its chest, and all of them with glowing purple eyes.

"I told you there were noises!" Nelly growled. "But no! No one listens to Nelly because she's not a boy, and doesn't have a fancy gauntlet or a flashy knife or a big, heavy hammer!"

"Big, heavy hammer!" repeated the automatons, as they closed in on Barthian, Salmon and Nelly.

Barthian looked from one automaton to the other, realizing that there were far too many of them to fight off. "We're trapped! There's no way out!"

"No way out!" shouted the nearest automaton.

"No way out! No way out! No way out!"

CHAPTER ELEVEN

SALMON TOOK A swing with his hammer, narrowly missing the head of an automaton.

"Ooh!" the automaton said.

"Ooh!" the rest of the automatons echoed.

"No, stop!" shouted Nelly. "Listen to me!"

"It'd better be good, Chops!" Salmon shouted back.

"There's something different about these automatons," Nelly said. "They're not trying to hurt us."

"Hurt us! Hurt us!"

"No!" said Nelly, looking around at the automatons. "We're not trying to hurt you...and you're not trying to hurt us."

"Hurt us! Hurt us!"

Nelly rolled her eyes and slapped her hand against her brow. One of the automatons stepped forward.

"What's your name?" Nelly asked.

"No name," answered the automaton.

"No name! No name!"

"Why are you here? Where are you from?"

"From Evercity. The court of the Emperor."

At the mention of the Emperor, the automatons said "Oooh!" together, and bowed their heads.

"What class of automaton are you?" Barthian asked.

"Whippers!" said the automaton speaking to Nelly.

"Whippers! Whippers!" half the automatons repeated.

Another one stepped forward.

"Snappers!" it said.

"Snappers! Snappers!"

"Whippers and Snappers!" said Salmon. "That's clever! Whipper-Snappers!"

"Whipper-Snappers! Whipper-Snappers!"

"Servants of the Emperor!" the first Whipper-Snapper said. "Children of the Emperor."

"Children! Children!"

"Why are you here?" Nelly asked again. "Did you run away from Evercity?"

"Emperor is cruel," the automaton said. "Emperor is angry. Emperor is unkind."

"See!" Nelly said to Salmon. "They're on our side!"

"Our side! Our side!"

Barthian approached the automaton. He had a lot of questions, but some were more important than others.

"Why are your eyes purple? And where are your fog boilers?"

"Ooh," said the automaton. "Aether!"

"Aether! Aether!"

"Aether?" Salmon repeated. "Aether is an olden days myth."

"Aether is true," the automaton said.

"Aether is true! Aether is true!"

Barthian had a closer look at the automaton's chassis. On its back, in place of a fog boiler, was a small device that resembled the animus servo. It was made of copper and the frame was covered in runes Barthian didn't recognize and couldn't decipher. At its centre was a spherical container, about the size of his palm, filled with a purple substance. It wasn't a liquid, and it wasn't a gas. It was something in between. It was in constant motion, swirling, ebbing, and flowing, like the surface of a river when a gentle eddy has been created by the water's movement among the rocks. Barthian thought of the Pool of Stars, how it seemed to be alive and in constant motion as it threw light around the smugglers cave.

"I've never seen anything like this. Who made this device?" Barthian asked.

"Ooh, secret!" said the automaton.

Barthian tried not to show his frustration at the vague answer, and persisted.

"Was it the Emperor? Did this happen in Evercity?"

"Not the Emperor!" the automaton said.

"Not the Emperor! Not the Emperor!"

But…that left only one possibility. Barthian was almost afraid to ask: "Is this old tech?"

"Old tech!"

"Old tech! Old tech!"

"That can't be true," Salmon said. "These automatons belonged to the Emperor. There hasn't been old tech in Evercity since before the Emperor, if it existed even then."

"It exists now!" Barthian said. "It's here, in front of your eyes!"

"Where is the aether from?" said Nelly.

"Aether Swell!"

"Aether Swell! Aether Swell!"

"What's Aether Swell?" Barthian asked.

It was Salmon who answered: "Aether Swell is up beyond the old Everbright Manor—the crystal caverns, bursting from the foot of the Old Mount."

At the mention of the name Everbright, the automatons became agitated and began stamping their feet up and down. Salmon raised his hammer again.

"No!" shouted Nelly. "They're dancing!"

Barthian looked around at the ring of Whipper-Snappers, each one doing the same thing but in their own way. Nelly was right—they were dancing.

"Everbright!" sang the automaton. "Everbright! Everbright!"

"Everbright! Everbright!"

The automaton took another step forward, not towards Nelly, but towards Barthian. Salmon raised his hammer arm defensively.

"It's all right," Barthian assured him. "They won't hurt us."

The automaton raised its hand and placed its palm, gently and almost reverently, on Barthian's chest. Its hand felt warm, and the automaton's eyes glowed brightly.

"Everbright," it whispered, and the whisper was echoed around the circle.

"Everbright. Everbright."

"Spooky!" said Salmon. "No wonder people think this place is haunted."

"What does it mean?" Nelly asked, putting a hand on Barthian's arm.

"I don't know," Barthian admitted. "Maybe he's telling us to go the Everbright Manor."

"Everbright," the automaton said again, gently tapping Barthian's chest.

"Yes," Barthian said to the automaton, nodding. "We will go."

"Yes," said the automaton, also nodding. "Everbright."

"Everbright! Everbright!"

"Before we go anywhere we need to rest," Salmon said. "The manor is a few hours away. Beyond that is the Boomlands…and then the forest."

"Rest!" the automaton said.

"Rest! Rest!" echoed the others, and they slowly began to disperse.

Not all of them dispersed, though. Several automatons remained and took up positions to keep watch. Two stood guard over by the steps. The first Whipper-Snapper stayed close as well, and when Barthian, Salmon, and Nelly lay down near the fire, the automaton lay down beside them, and purred gently like a cat as they nodded off, finally feeling warm and safe.

When day broke, Barthian was gently woken by the automaton tapping on his shoulder. His sleep had been deep and full of dreams, of a large house and an automaton with glowing purple eyes. It was difficult for him to wake up, and if their mission wasn't so urgent and time so critical, Barthian felt like he could have stayed at Mill Stone for longer, chatting to the automatons about Evercity and the Emperor, and the mystery person who had converted them from servants fuelled by fogtech, to free automatons powered by aether.

But he remembered Germain and felt a sudden pang of sorrow. Time was critical indeed—it could mean the difference between Germain surviving, and Germain…Barthian couldn't bring himself to think about it. His feelings were so mixed. On the one hand, he felt that the journey had opened his eyes to the land and history of Aethasia, and a sudden hunger burned within him to discover more—about his own past, about the distant past, and about such mysteries as aether, the Great Engineer, the Emperor, and Evercity.

But on the other, his sense of adventure was tempered by his constant worry, and by the ever-present dread that unless he made it home soon his father wouldn't make it.

"Come on!" Barthian said, shaking Salmon by the shoulder. "We need to go. I have to get the Aether Rose—today!"

Nelly moaned when Barthian shook her awake. "Not yet, Barty, I need more sleep! I'm too tired! What if I stay here and you come get me on the way back? We can't just leave these automatons, anyway."

"We can't do that!" Salmon said, even as Barthian considered her idea. "If this journey's showed us anything, it's that we have to expect the unexpected."

"What does that mean?" Barthian asked.

"It means we don't know if we'll be coming back."

Salmon was right, and Barthian knew it. Perhaps Nelly knew it, deep inside, which is why she preferred to stay in Mill Stone with the Whipper-Snappers.

When their goodbyes finally came, Barthian was reluctant to leave the automatons as well. And while the automatons didn't feel emotions like Barthian, Nelly and Salmon did, they looked despondent at their leaving.

"We'll come and see you again," said a tearful Nelly, standing at the steps to the ground floor of the old mill.

"Again!" said the automaton, and the word was echoed throughout the crowd of automatons that had gathered to see them off.

"Again! Again!"

At that, they set out again towards the east, with the new day's sun at their backs and fresh determination in their hearts, despite the sad farewell.

"I wonder what today will bring," said Barthian, setting his sights on the foot of the Old Mount.

⌁

What the day brought was an open road and sunshine, a clear blue sky with white clouds, and a light breeze that blew across the land from the ocean in the far distance to their left. At Salmon's insistence, they followed the top road from Mill Stone, which took them up through the lower steppes towards the mountain. It was a tougher walk than the low road and seemed to climb and climb throughout the morning as they slowly made their way east. But Salmon was adamant that the low road was dangerous, and Barthian decided to trust him, since he knew so much about other things. If it wasn't the bandits then it was the Emperor's automatons, which made regular patrols of the low road to ward off anyone with intentions of entering the Giant Seed Forest through the Boomlands.

"The Emperor is building his new flagship," Salmon reminded them. "He'll have increased his patrols on the highway, no doubt about that."

Salmon proved to be right. As they climbed higher towards the foot of the Old Mount, they had an unbroken view of the flatlands to the ocean, of the River of Bones weaving its way east towards Everbright Quay, and of the road they would have taken if Barthian and Nelly had had their way. Not once, but twice, they watched as a heavily armed patrol made its way down the forest road, combing the land for would-be intruders such as them.

"Look at them," said Salmon, marveling at the show of force.

"Bombardiers and Pacifiers, Combustonauts and Lashers. Techno Mites, Autofficers…they've got the lot."

Barthian marveled too, and secretly suspected the patrols had increased not only because of the airship the Emperor was building at the Echo Factory, but because he and his friends were still on the loose. Cleverley had sent word, after all, and Barthian was sure Grimm would not call off his henchman until the watch had been returned.

They pressed on, as the sun climbed higher and their shadows on the road got shorter and shorter, and eventually disappeared entirely. They had walked the entire morning. Their feet were sore, their heads were hot, and their bellies were hungry and noisy.

"It must be time to stop and eat," Nelly said.

"We have nothing left," Barthian said, apologetically.

"Nothing? Absolutely nothing?"

"We have a potato. But apart from that, absolutely nothing. I thought we'd be there by now, eating fruit in the forest and drinking clean spring water. I didn't count on a kidnapper wasting so much of our time."

"Can we at least rest?" asked Nelly, whose feet were swollen and sore and covered in blisters.

"Not yet, but very soon," Salmon pointed ahead. "Look!"

Up ahead, through a gap in the trees, Barthian saw what Salmon had already spotted: a great cluster of purple spikes, both large and small, rising from the ground at different angles, refracting the midday sun and throwing rainbow rays of colourful, magical light in every direction.

"What is it?" Nelly breathed, her mouth agape.

"It's the Aether Swell," Barthian said, transfixed.

Salmon stared at Barthian. "How did you know that?"

"I've seen it before." Barthian knew this would sound crazy—it even sounded crazy to him—but he also knew that he *had* seen this before.

"I thought you'd never been outside No Man's Landing!" Nelly protested.

"I—I didn't think I had," Barthian answered. "But I've definitely seen this before. And from this very spot, too."

"You must have dreamt it," said Salmon. "Or heard people describe it."

"Maybe," Barthian admitted. "But it's very familiar. Maybe Father brought me here once."

The closer they got to the Aether Swell, the more convinced Barthian became that this was no dream or constructed vision from other people's stories. He had been here long ago, back before...before what? He couldn't remember details of this place, or the faces of people he was with, but he remembered the feeling: the giddiness, the wonder, the intrigue. He remembered gazing for what seemed like forever at the crystal caves, at the sheer size and beauty and majesty of the natural formations.

As they approached the edge of the cavernous opening in the mountain, beneath the giant spray of crystals, Barthian broke into a run, and the others followed. He stopped abruptly on the very lip, looking down into a vast gorge of aether crystal bursting out from the ground like wild flowers, except like no flowers any of them had ever seen. The crystals were of all shapes and sizes, some taller than the tallest buildings in No Man's Landing, others as small as the automatons they had left behind in Mill Stone; in clusters and pairs, single spires, or like the spiky skin of a Snowmoorian cactus ice flower. In among the crystals, tunnels bored into the mountainside—gateways down into the very heart of the Old Mount itself.

"It's beautiful," Nelly breathed.

"It makes me feel funny inside," said Salmon.

"Me too!" Barthian admitted.

The truth was, it made him feel strong...and light...and happy. He wanted to run and play. He wanted to eat. He wanted to gaze up at the sun with his eyes closed and his mouth open. He wanted to go with his friends and explore in the Aether Swell tunnels.

But, he reminded himself, he had to press on towards the Giant Seed Forest, to find the Aether Rose and return to No Man's Landing, without delay.

"They say there are things living in it," said Salmon.

"In the tunnels?" Nelly asked, pulling an expression of disbelief.

"The crystal. They say it's alive."

"They say that because it grows," said Nelly.

"The Aether looked alive in that device on the back of the Whipper-Snappers," Barthian said.

"Maybe it's alive now, listening to us."

"That's silly," said Nelly.

"You still think you've been here before?" Salmon asked Barthian.

"I know I have," Barthian said.

Barthian looked up at the peak of the Old Mount in the near distance. It was the closest they had come to the slopes of the mountain itself, and it rose majestically towards the sun, its snowy cap glimmering and shimmering in the light of midday. Then he looked down the steppes of the Aether Swell, through the tree-covered slopes towards the sea.

And there, beyond the woods, was the roof of Everbright Manor, and beyond the house were the overgrown gardens, the forest road, and the Everbright Quay.

"They are all linked," he said.

"What are?" said Salmon.

"The mountain," Barthian said, pointing. "The Aether Swell. The house."

"Linked, how?" Nelly asked.

"I don't know," Barthian admitted. "Let's head down to the house and see if we can find out."

⁂

Even before they walked into the manor through the busted front doors, Barthian knew he had been here before as well. He remembered that the doors would magically open up, drawn aside by machines in the walls. As they walked through into the great hall he remembered the broken down and dusty old engines against the walls and the enormous candelabra hanging from the ceiling—only he remembered them being in their original condition before the decay set in. He knew the layout of the second floor before they mounted the grand stairs, and had flashes of running from bedroom to bedroom chasing…something. He couldn't remember. But he remembered the excitement, the giggling, the dizziness that comes when all the fun overheats your head and you have to stop suddenly because you're out of breath and in desperate need of a drink.

He remembered faces too. Not Germain's, strangely, but a man and a woman. He remembered hearing shouts and cries and seeing, for the first time, the look of fear in their eyes. There was something else: a small automaton, cheeky and wise, dancing on the spot like the Whipper-Snappers in Mill Stone. It was a Techno Mite with a big old welding mask for a face, and a wide grille for a mouth that made it look as though it was constantly grinning. Barthian called it…

The memory was almost there, but not quite. It was as if the house—or maybe it was the Aether Swell—was bringing all these memories out from his fog-muddled mind. There was no hint of the fog anywhere in the manor or in the grounds. Maybe it was like the old myths said, that the aether pushed the fog back from Aethasia. Maybe it pushed the fog back from people's minds as well, because these were memories Barthian had never had in his mind before. Even Nelly and Salmon were convinced when he told them what they would find in rooms they hadn't gone into yet.

"I just don't know how you could have been here before," said Nelly.

"I think I may have lived here for a while," Barthian said.

He told them about the Techno Mite, and how they played hid-ey-hidey through the Manor, and how the automaton would remain with him through the night, protecting him from scary things.

"What sort of scary things?" Salmon said.

"I don't know," said Barthian.

Upstairs, in a small bedroom—one of three that looked out over the gardens and the front gates—was a dusty old wardrobe in which they found a big chest full of clothes. They pulled everything out and Nelly found a coat that was much better than the one she was wear-ing. Salmon found a large leather belt that wrapped twice around his waist, and Barthian dug out a scarlet, hooded cloak. It had the name EVERBRIGHT stitched in gold along the inside hem, and although it was much too big for any of them to wear, Barthian shoved it in his sack as a souvenir.

On the ground floor, at the rear of the Manor, down a long hallway from the main entrance hall, a big family room housing a fireplace constructed of big slabs of stone with a large wooden mantle over it led to a family kitchen, and beyond the kitchen a cold larder. There they found food—not fresh food, but not terribly old food either. There were potatoes, yams, and carrots. There was a small cask of salted meat as well, and a pot of flour and jar of olive oil. They ate from the carrots and the meat and before too long they had filled themselves right up.

"You know what this means?" Salmon asked.

"That someone has been living here," Barthian said.

"Perhaps they're still living here," Nelly suggested.

Salmon examined the fireplace in the big room next to the kitchen and found an iron poker lying nearby with no dust on it. "Probably vagabonds or vagrants," he said. "The Emperor has outlawed anyone living here since the Usurping, but that wouldn't stop travelers or bandits using it for a night or two to hide from the patrols."

Salmon was convincing, but even so, Barthian was nervous. Nelly picked up on his nervousness and moved closer to him.

"I think we should leave," she said.

"I do too," Barthian said. "We need to get to the Boomlands before dusk so I can find that Aether Rose before nightfall."

They filled Barthian's sack with as many of the vegetables as he could carry and prepared to head out through the front doors, but the shuffling of feet in the hallway froze them in their tracks. Salmon put his finger to his lips.

A second sound followed: the flutter of wings and the chirp of a happy bird. A mechanised voice said something indecipherable out in the entrance hall—an automaton!

"Wait here," Barthian whispered, and he crept to the door.

"What are you doing?" whispered Nelly, but Barthian gestured with his hand to quiet her.

He leant his head out into the hallway and peered around the door. The grand staircase blocked his view, so he took a step more and leaned even further over until his head almost touched the opposite wall. He could see the back of a small automaton, a Techno Mite, standing in the hall and looking out over the gardens toward the front gates. On its back was a boiler, but not a fog boiler. It was full of purple aether, swirling and excitable like the aether in the devices back at Mill Stone. On the Techno Mite's shoulder was a small, mechanised bird, about the size and shape of a song thrush. It chirped excitedly, dancing on the spot, and annoying the little Techno Mite.

"My requests, they mean so little?" the automaton said, and gave an automated "Bzzt" at the end.

The bird chirped.

"You can fly anywhere in the house—bzzt—but no, it has to be on the shoulder."

Another chirp.

"Disappointing."

Chirp.

"Troubling."

Chirp.

"Fatal."

The bird lifted its wings and fluttered away from the Techno Mite, flying several circuits around the candelabra before floating back down to the Techno Mite's other shoulder.

"Not funny. Bzzt," said the automaton.

And suddenly Barthian remembered its name.

"Click-Clack!" he shouted, and ran down the hall towards the Techno Mite, which squealed with fright, turned on its heels and ran with stumpy little legs back into the front drawing room. The mechanised bird followed.

Barthian skidded to a halt in the hall, but slipped on the dusty wooden floor and fell over onto his side. He heard another squeal from Click-Clack, who had hidden in a big cupboard against the far wall of the drawing room.

"Barthian!" Nelly shouted, pointing out the front door towards the gates. "Look!"

Barthian looked where she pointed and saw a figure pushing open the gates and coming into the manor grounds

Salmon pulled down his goggles and adjusted the frames until the figure came into sharper focus.

"It's the hooded man," he said. "He's coming this way!"

Chapter Twelve

"Don't argue, Tick-Tock!" Salmon said, holding open the door from the conservatory to the grounds behind the house.

"I'm not going!" said Barthian, standing obstinately in the doorway. "Not without you two!"

"He's right, Barty," Nelly said. "You have to. You have to go now!"

There wasn't a moment to lose, Salmon insisted. Barthian needed to run, as fast as he possibly could, up to the top road, while Salmon and Nelly kept the hooded man pinned down in the house. If Barthian was quick, and if Salmon and Nelly had their wits about them, he would put enough distance between himself and the hooded man to reach the Boomlands before the hooded man caught up with him.

"What about you?" Barthian said. "You're in terrible danger!"

"It's you he wants, Tick-Tock," said Salmon. "And that blasted watch. Now, go!"

Salmon gave Barthian a shove, and without pausing to say goodbye or good luck, or any of the things that Aethasians say to one another when they have time for a long, drawn out goodbye, Barthian jumped from the top step and ran off through the grounds back towards the Aether Swell. If he could make the top road while Salmon and Nelly kept the hooded man searching through the manor, he could make his way quickly down to the Boomlands and into the Giant Seed Forest.

If not...

But Barthian wasn't thinking about "if"s. He was thinking about running and keeping his head down, and about how every single step took him ever closer to his goal. He ducked in between the trees at the end of Everbright gardens and disappeared into the undergrowth, weaving through patches of shrubbery and leaping over streams. He followed the path they had taken down from Aether Swell, running on instinct as much as memory, sniffing his way through the woods and up the steppes of the Old Mount.

He didn't stop until he couldn't take another single step without taking a breath. That was the first time he dared to look back.

He had made more ground than he thought, and already the manor looked like a small toy in the distance. There was no sign of the hooded man, near the house or in the woods. That didn't mean much though, Barthian realised. The hooded man might have overpowered Salmon and Nelly quickly. If so, he might be hard on Barthian's tail even as he stood there getting the air back in his chest. So, Barthian turned and ran some more, and didn't pause again until he'd reached the road to the Boomlands.

There he stopped, crouched, and hid in the bushes. He calmed his breathing and just listened. His hearing was sharper than normal, and he wondered whether the Aether Swell had cleared his ears like it cleared his memory. But all he heard was the sound of the breeze through the woods, the chirping of birds, and the rustling sounds of the hedgerows as rabbits and other creatures foraged for food. Only when he was fully convinced that he wasn't being followed did Barthian set out on the road, hurrying but not running, down towards the Giant Seed Forest, which was already in view at the foot of the mountain.

Barthian emerged from the trees and stood at the edge of the Emperor's forest defense—a wide swath of land from which every tree and shrub had been removed, and the land itself torn up so that nothing would ever grow there again. To make certain, a network of burners spewed fog across the landscape all day 'round, and it covered the Boomlands like a mist, hovering at knee level as it did in No Man's Landing, suffocating the soil and marking the land with the Emperor's unique stamp.

But Barthian could handle the fog. He'd grown up with it, after all. What he hadn't encountered before were the Boomers themselves— huge, floating mines, with explosive spikes that made them look like the outer casing of a chestnut skin, and tethered to the ground by monstrous chains. Some of the boomers floated high, as high as the clouds, while others floated just above head height, shielding the Echo Factory from attacks from the air, and from the ground. There were too many of them to count, each one strategically placed across the Boomlands to make certain every possible path to Giant Seed Forest was defended.

Barthian picked up a large rock, and threw it as far into the Boomlands as he could. The movement triggered a Boomer, which swept down from the sky in a graceful arc and caught the rock with one of its spikes, which exploded on impact, incinerating the rock. The Boomer continued its sweep and rose back into the air, ending right where it started, as if nothing had happened.

"So that's how it works," Barthian mused. "It's clockwork."

Each Boomer was powered the same as a clock, with cogs and springs and a mechanism that was always ready to fire in response to the slightest bit of movement in the field below. Barthian could hear the mechanism whirring into gear, so attuned were his ears to the workings of timepieces. It made sense to Barthian that each boomer was triggered like clockwork. It meant the Boomers were ready to strike any time of day or night. It also meant they had to follow certain patterns, and if Barthian's ears were attuned as well as he thought they were, he might predict the movement of each one before it swept down from the sky.

That was the theory, anyway.

There was only one way to test it. With time running out for Germain back in No Man's Landing, there was no time like the present. Barthian had to walk across the Boomlands.

He closed his eyes to steady his nerves. His palms were sweaty and his heart was skipping beats. His legs felt like jelly. One wrong move and he would be blasted into a hundred pieces, scattered over the Boomlands and left to rot. He took a deep breath, and remembered how he'd felt at the Aether Swell—the unexpected courage, the hope that rose up inside him despite the challenges that he, Nelly, and Salmon had confronted. He felt the same courage rise up in him again.

He knew that he would see his father again, that they would talk about the things he had discovered, and the things he had remembered. He would ask Germain about the Everbright Manor, about Click-Clack and the Aether Swell, and he would ask him the one question that was burning most fiercely in his mind: Where was Germain when all that was happening?

Barthian took the first step, and listened to the whirring of a clockwork mechanism as the first boomer prepared to sweep down out of the sky.

⁊

A spiral spring inside the boomer unfurled and triggered a series of gears, which powered the boomer's crankshaft. Barthian heard it, clear as a bird calling out in the woods. Then there was a click as the reticulated spline engaged and the gearing mechanism brought the boomer out of the sky. Barthian stepped aside, just far enough that the boomer swept past him, but not so far that he triggered another boomer. Not yet anyway.

He jumped forward, and heard the whirring of a spiral spring again. Another boomer swept down to catch him with its explosive nodes. This one came within inches, and he felt the wind rush past him as it swept by.

Another jump, another boomer. If the whirring of the clockwork mechanism inside the floating mines came from Barthian's left, he jumped to the right. If it came from the right, he jumped to the left. Meanwhile, every jump took him just that little bit closer to the forest. But it was agonisingly slow, and for the most part it felt like he wasn't advancing at all, as if he was crawling through shifting sand on the edges of the beach at Smuggler's Cove. But there was no turning back now. When he was ready to give up and just lie down right there in the mine field, he thought of his father, at home in his bed, struggling to breathe, his chest aching from the green lung that assaulted his body. And so Barthian would move again, and advance just that little bit more.

Jump. *Whir. Click. Engage. Swoop.* Jump. *Whir. Click. Engage. Swoop.* Jump…

Barthian reached the halfway point and stopped. He was exhausted, and the exhaustion was playing tricks with his ears. Was the whirring coming from the left, or from the right? Should he jump this way or that? One bad decision, one poor jump, and it was all over. But the midway point was the most important and most critical place to be. It meant that going back would take as long and was just as risky as moving forward, so there was nothing else to do but keep going, keep his eyes on the giant trees of the forest ahead, and try to focus, focus, focus, on the sounds, the movement, the rhythms. Barthian took just one look back…and saw Salmon and Nelly emerging from the trees.

Barthian dared not call out to them in case the Boomers could be triggered by sound as well as motion, and he couldn't wave at them. So he stood there, unable to move one way or the other, desperately wishing he was still with his friends, who he now noticed had a small automaton with them.

Click-Clack…

Salmon was waving, and so was Nelly. They couldn't hear the clock-work the way he could, and if they decided to step out and follow him…

He couldn't think about it. He had to go back. He had to keep them from trying to follow him. But then another figure emerged from the trees: the hooded man. Salmon and Nelly stopped waving, and didn't take another step.

So that was it. They were his captives. And Click-Clack too.

Barthian turned to face the forest, and decided not to look back at his friends again, for fear it would mess with his head and make the rest of the crossing fatal. But he felt their long glare as he took another step and narrowly avoided another swooping boomer. Then another. And another. There were tears building up in his eyes now. Tears of exhaustion, and of doubt, but mainly tears of loneliness. And helpless-ness. He had brought Nelly along for the ride. He had allowed Salmon to come along with them. It was all his fault. And now there wasn't a thing he could do to help them.

Just one more step. Then another. Almost there. Almost…

Barthian emerged from the Boomlands and collapsed to the ground, his heart thundering and his chest finally able to breathe freely. He looked behind him, at where Nelly and Salmon had stood, but they were gone. He was truly alone now—and his friends were Grimm's prisoners.

"I have to keep going," he said aloud. "Keep moving."

But ahead of him, the forest undergrowth was a wall of matted vegetation, dark and foreboding, blurred and twisted by the fog at the heart of the forest. The darkness of the forest itself was the Emperor's last line of defense, the stuff of every child's nightmares. Salmon had been right when he told Barthian that he would never confront any-thing like this. But Barthian reminded himself that all he needed to do was take one more step…and so into the forest he went.

There were paths everywhere. But not all paths went somewhere. Some ended in a boggy swamp, others in an impenetrable wall of trees and undergrowth, all damp and sticky from the putrid air that sat like a fever on the forest. From time to time he heard movement in the tops of the trees above him, but he never saw anything. The tops of the trees were so high that he couldn't even see where the forest broke through to the sky. Even so, he fancied that he saw people up there, tiny creatures no bigger than the Mill Stone Whipper-Snappers, and he wondered if they were hiding in the forest too.

Deeper into the forest the paths went, winding this way and that, then back around again. Always, he looked at the ground for signs of the Aether Rose, but couldn't believe that any such flower could survive in a place so dark, so riddled with fog. He tried not to lose heart but it was becoming increasingly grim, and he knew that he couldn't wander through the forest forever. If he didn't find the flower soon…

A clearing suddenly appeared up ahead, a small glade into which the late afternoon sun poured down in beams as the steam of the forest rose to meet it. Barthian edged forward, cautiously, such a place seemed unnatural and dangerous in a forest so dense and lifeless.

But there, growing in the centre of the glade, was the Aether Rose. Not one or two, but a whole carpet of them, rising up to meet the sunlight, and Barthian realised that it was the rose itself that kept the darkness of the forest at bay. Right here, in the dark heart of the Giant Seed Forest, a pure remnant of the old Aethasia was still present, still holding back the fog.

Barthian ran towards the light, and finally he was there, kneeling beside the rose, marveling at its beauty, not quite ready to believe that he had made it, he had reached his destination. He reached out to grab the flower.

"Halt!"

Barthian jumped, jerking back his hand, and raised his eyes to see a dozen automatons marching into the glade from the forest all around.

But these were not normal automatons. They had the appearance of Pacifiers and Troubleshooters, but looked as though they had been put together by a mad engineer intent on experimenting with which limbs could go with which bodies, and which heads would fit inside which helmets.

They wore human clothing, unlike the automatons Barthian had seen everywhere else. Not normal clothing like he saw on the townsfolk in No Man's Landing, but torn tunics and greatcoats with no sleeves, and sashes across their chests, and bandannas on their heads. Each one wielded a cutlass as well as the rifles and flame throwers they had welded to their artillery arms. In short, they looked like pirates. And sure enough, even as he formed that thought, a real life sky pirate stepped out from the trees, his pistols loaded and cocked and pointed right at Barthian.

"Lower the weapon!" he snapped. He was a small man with oily black hair that was swept back from his brow and hung below his shoulders. He wore a black tunic and pants and big black boots, as well as a waistcoat of thick, scratched black leather in the fashion of Salmon's Horizon People. Thin leather straps covered his forearms, wrists and knuckles like the street fighters who sometimes visited No Man's landing looking for coin. It was immediately obvious to Barthian that he wasn't someone he would ever consider messing with, so he lowered the gauntlet.

"The name's Wormwood," he sneered. "First mate on the sky pirateer, *The Lamentation*. You may have heard of it."

"I've seen it!" Barthian said, nodding.

"There's a price on your head," Wormwood continued, "and we wannit."

Barthian looked down at the bed of Aether Roses, growing wild and free in the sun-kissed glade, and realised this was his last chance to grab one. But as he knelt and grabbed for the nearest one he heard Wormwood shouting, "Take him, lads!" and felt an almighty whack on the back of his head.

Then darkness…and the return of a recurring nightmare, of crawling on all fours along a fog-filled tunnel that never ends.

CHAPTER THIRTEEN

BARTHIAN WOKE ALONE, in a cage below decks, in a storage hold full of crates and barrels. The space was dimly lit by fog lamps attached to the walls of the hold, so Barthian could make out a heavy iron door that he presumed was his only way out. But his gauntlet and sack were gone and the cage was heavily padlocked. Luckily, Grimm's watch was still in his pocket, but otherwise this was the end of the line.

The blow to Barthian's head had made him black out, but he remembered moments of being conscious and images that had stayed with him. A skiff had risen from the forest, a small dirigible powered by a great fog boiler and turbines, as Barthian lay on the deck surrounded by automaton pirates, and Wormwood sneering down on him.

Then he remembered a monstrous, black airship in the clouds, the same ship he saw with his father as they lay beside the Pool of Stars, a day that felt so long ago and so far, far away. Tall rigging fluttered in the wind, and the sails were black and threatening. The skiff came to land on the foredeck of *The Lamentation* as Barthian blacked out again, and found himself back in the tunnel of his nightmares.

Barthian heard a sound beyond the reinforced door—the click of a lock being turned, followed by heavy boots descending wooden steps. Then the door swung inward and Wormwood entered the hold, pausing for a moment to assess his captive from the doorway. Then he crouched down at the cage and eyeballed his prisoner.

"Sleep well, Master Barthian?"

Barthian said nothing, but rubbed the back of his head where the pain was most intense.

"Oh, the head. My lads get a bit—feisty, from time to time."

Barthian averted his gaze. Wormwood's eyes were black and deep and mean, and Barthian didn't want them staring into his eyes, seeing how weak and vulnerable he felt.

"You'll be comfortable here," Wormwood said, testing the bars of the cage. "Lots of time to…think."

"Where are you taking me?" Barthian demanded, raising his face to look at the pirate again.

"You, my boy, are going to the Isle."

"The Isle?"

"That's where Grimm is. And Grimm's the one with the coin."

"You're selling me to Grimm?"

"Fair bit of coin for a fair day's work."

"There's nothing fair about it."

"You're a fugitive, lad. Pirates are good citizens, doing the Emperor's bidding. Doing him a favour! And getting a bit of coin for it. It's how Aethasia works."

"How much coin will you get?"

"More than you've conceived of!" Wormwood's eyes sparked. He flashed a nasty grin, revealing broken and blackened teeth. He smelt of tobacco and garlic and his breath reeked.

"What if I worked for you—here, on the ship?" Barthian asked, more desperately than he'd intended.

"Earn your freedom?"

"Yes!"

"No vacancies right now," Wormwood said. "Not for children, anyway."

"I'm the timekeeper's apprentice. Have you no clocks that I can fix?"

Wormwood put one hand on his hip and tapped his chin with a finger of the other hand. "Hm, let me think…no!"

"None at all?"

"We don't go by clocks or clockwork. We're pirates!"

"So how do you keep time?"

"We don't keep time," Wormwood snapped. "We're pirates!"

Wormwood shoved a great, brass key in the big padlock and unlocked the door of the cage. Then he reached in and grabbed Barthian by the collar, hauling him out like cargo.

"Are we there already?" Barthian asked. He would have preferred to stay in the cage.

"Not for ages. But Captain Gall wants to see you."

"Maybe he'll give me a job?"

"Hmm, I wonder." It was the same sarcastic tone he'd used before.

Barthian sighed. "He won't, will he?"

"No, he won't!"

Wormwood pushed Barthian ahead of him, up the steep, narrow steps to the main deck. Then he prodded him forward along the narrow gangways of the ship, which weren't much bigger than the tunnel that plagued Barthian's dreams—dark and close, poorly lit by feeble fog lamps fixed to the wooden paneling on the walls. It was like a cave and Barthian suspected they were going deeper into the heart of *The Lamentation*, right into the heart of the pirate's lair.

The captain's quarters were behind an ornate door that swung inwards to a low room with no windows, just multiple fog lamps burning on the walls, in keeping with the gangways. At one end of the room was a large desk, and at the other, a long table made from a huge slab of hard wood. Several crates and barrels sat around the table as chairs, and the captain perched on one of these at the head, with his back to the wall, looking out over the room. When Barthian entered he stood, flicked his wavy white hair away from his eyes and strode to Barthian with his hand extended.

Barthian wasn't sure what he was supposed to do, so he reached out and shook the hand.

The captain sighed, looking equal parts annoyed and disappointed. He quickly shook himself out of it, though.

"Salutations!" he said, in a voice that danced and sang. It was not what Barthian expected. "Delighted to meet you! I've heard so much—actually, not much at all. I have no idea. Sit down and tell me all about it."

Barthian sat on a chest as Wormwood stayed by the door, blocking any hope of escape. Gall returned to the head of the table.

"Well," he said. "Don't be shy!"

"Erm…" Barthian fidgeted with his hands, unsure what exactly he was supposed to be telling Gall about.

Gall shot an angry look across the room. "What have you done to the poor boy, Wormwood?"

"Nothing, boss," Wormwood said, shrugging.

"He's scared witless!"

"He also had a nasty blow to the back of the head, boss."

"From whom?!" said Gall, his voice rising to a high squeal as he jumped to his feet.

"From one of the lads."

"An auto?"

"Yes, boss."

"Which one?"

"I'd rather not …"

"Wormwood, tell me!" said Gall, menacingly.

"That one that wears bandages over one side of its face."

"I'm not sure…"

"He's got them big goggles that he wears."

"Oh yes, I know the one. Throw him off the ship!"

Wormwood started. "Boss?"

"You heard me! Throw him off the ship. Not right now, of course, but as soon as we're done. Throw him off!"

"Yes, boss."

"Now," Gall said, turning back to Barthian. "Tell me about this little pretty." Barthian's gauntlet was on the table, beside his sack. Gall picked it up and examined the nodes and palm trigger, and the gyro beneath the wrist. "Here, you can have that back," Gall said, tossing Barthian the sack. "But this…I'm keeping this pretty."

"It's a weapon," said Barthian.

"Oh, I can see that," Gall said. "What does it do?"

Barthian looked to Wormwood, then back at Gall.

"It shoots lightning."

"It never does!" Gall's eyes widened as he grinned.

Barthian nodded.

"Show me!"

Barthian blinked. "Sorry?"

"Show me what it does!"

"Here?"

"Yes, why not?"

"Ahem," Wormwood interrupted.

Gall rolled his eyes. "What is it, Wormwood?"

"I've an idea, boss."

"Well? Spill it!"

"What if he demonstrates the weapon on the auto, boss?"

"The one with the bandages? And the goggles?"

"The very one."

"Marvelous!" Gall clapped his hands and giggled. "Your best idea in days, Wormwood. Let's go find it."

Gall sprang to his feet. He had the gauntlet in his hands and marched with it past Wormwood, who fell in behind Barthian and nudged him to keep up with the captain. Eventually they emerged onto the foredeck of the airship and Barthian copped a blast of icy wind as he was suddenly exposed to the skies above Aethasia.

To the starboard side he could see out over the seas, almost as far as the mythical Nautilina and the Ends of the Earth Falls. To the port side, the peak of the Old Mount was so close that Barthian felt he could reach out and scoop up some snow. He walked out onto the deck, where the automaton pirates were lounging, or playing card games, or arm wrestling.

Behind him, the ship looked like a great haunted mansion in the sky, with leaning towers and turrets, rising up from the front of the airship to back. Like all Aethasian airships, its belly was a great dirigible that kept it floating in the sky. All around the ship, windows glowed with a dull green light from the fog boilers installed throughout the entire structure. At the rear of the ship, he could make out not one but three enormous propellers, and around the hull multiple oil and fire cannons, armed and ready to douse and burn their enemies.

"This the one?" the captain called to Wormwood from over near the bow of the ship. He had his hands on the automaton with the bandages and the goggles.

"Yes, boss, that's the one!"

"Come with me, you," Gall said, and yanked the automaton from its card game and dragged it to the centre of the deck. Then he tossed the gauntlet to Barthian and told him to put it on.

"Do your thing!" he said, when Barthian was ready.

Barthian stared at his weapon in shock, certain it must be a trap. "My thing?"

"Yes, don't be a sap! Your thing! Fire lightning at the automaton that hurt you."

"Really?"

"YES!" said Gall. "Wormwood, give him a kick in the pants!"

Wormwood kicked Barthian hard on the backside with his big boots.

"Do it!" shouted Gall. "Let me see lightning!" and he raised his hands to the sky as if that's where the bolt would come from.

For a moment Barthian considered firing at either Gall or Wormwood—they had practically asked for it, after all—but there were too many crew members. He would quickly be overpowered and probably killed.

"All right," he said, as much to himself as to Wormwood or Gall. He took aim at the automaton and hit the palm trigger, and an arc of powerful blue light bolted from the nodes on the gauntlet and caught the automaton in its chest.

"WHOA—YES!" shouted Gall, clapping and jumping as the automaton clattered across the deck in several pieces. "I love it! I really love it!"

He skipped towards Barthian, still clapping.

"Let me have a go! Wormwood, we need a hundred of these! Are they mail order or store sale only?"

Barthian was about to take the gauntlet from his wrist when there was a sudden clanging of a bell up high on one of *The Lamentation*'s turrets. Wormwood and Gall looked about them at the sky and Barthian followed their gazes, because bells like that usually indicated DANGER or ATTACK or SOMETHING ELSE.

"Captain!" an automaton shouted from up high. "The Emperor's skiff!"

Over on the port side, between *The Lamentation* and the Old Mount, a small transport skiff rose up from the clouds and pulled alongside the pirate ship. It was flying the Emperor's flag, a large green X.

"Slow the ship!" Wormwood shouted. "Time for coin!" And then, to the automaton nearest to him: "Hold the boy!"

The airship slowed to a halt as the giant turbines reversed thrust. The Emperor's skiff came to a halt as well, as several crew of *The Lamentation* drew it alongside with grapple hooks, which was standard for a parlay. Barthian waited, trying to hide his shaking, knowing that this really was the end of the journey for him, and wondering whether it would be the Emperor himself who showered Wormwood and Gall with coin, or Grimm.

But the figure that emerged from the skiff wasn't the Emperor at all. It wasn't even Grimm.

It was the hooded man. He'd caught up with Barthian at last.

The hooded man raised his pistols and leveled them at Wormwood and Gall. The captain was immediately and suitably miffed.

"Steady on, old chap!" Gall said, sticking out his chest and putting his nose in the air at the nerve of this stranger to produce a weapon. "We're all on the same side!"

"I'm on no man's side. Hand over the boy!" It was the first time Barthian had heard the hooded man's voice, and it was gruff and determined, though somewhat muffled by the black cloth he had wrapped around the lower half of his face. His eyes were hidden by aviator goggles.

"That's what we're about to do, if you'll let us!" whined Gall. "Boy, over here!"

"Not so fast!" said Wormwood, stepping forward to block Barthian's path. "Until coin is tossed in our direction, the boy belongs to us."

The automaton holding onto Barthian tightened its grip.

"You stay right where you are!" Wormwood said, pointing to Barthian. He had a pistol tucked into his breeches at the small of his back, and his right hand angled slowly towards it.

"I concur, actually," said Gall, flicking back his hair and pointing his chin outward and upward. "We found the boy fair and square. He's ours. If the Emperor wants him, the Emperor can pay for him!"

"I don't speak for the Emperor!" said the hooded man.

"Same goes for Grimm!" said Gall, not giving in. "If Grimm wants the boy so badly, well, Grimm can shower us with coin! We're pirates, if you hadn't noticed. It's how we earn our keep!"

"I don't come from Grimm, either!"

This was a surprise, not just to Wormwood and Gall but to Barthian as well. But if the hooded man wasn't from Grimm, who had sent him?

Wormwood was apparently wondering the same thing. "You have no reward for us, that's my guess!" he bellowed, swaggering forward.

"You guess correctly," the hooded man said.

"Then we have no need to parlay," said Gall. "A quick word of advice, hooded creature: your best course of action is to hop back on board the Emperor's skiff, which you've obviously stolen from the Echo Factory, and be on your way."

"My captain is being very generous," Wormwood said. "Me, not so much."

"Ah yes, Wormwood, I thought you might have an addendum," Gall said.

"I certainly do, boss."

"Care to share it with the rest of us?"

"Certainly, boss."

Instantly, Wormwood whipped the pistol from his breeches and aimed it at the hooded man. Around the deck, a dozen or so pirate automatons, mangled and disfigured, raised their artillery and aimed it at the hooded man as well. He was completely outgunned.

"My offer is this," said Wormwood. "Lower your weapons, hand over your stolen skiff, and let my lovely pirates take you below decks."

The hooded man silently weighed the offer. Barthian could see him calculating the outcomes. His head leaned one way, then leaned the other, and he glanced around the deck taking the measure of his opposition.

"Barthian!" he called out. "I'm a friend of your father's, the timekeeper."

Barthian stood motionless, suddenly unsure of not only himself but everything else as well. He'd been afraid of the hooded man for so long, but now…he didn't know what to believe.

"Grimm had your father on the Isle," the hooded man continued. "But your father escaped and he's in hiding."

"Lies, boy," said Gall. "You can tell just by looking at him. The man's a pirate if ever I saw one."

"Takes one to know one, eh boss?" Wormwood asked.

"Precisely!" said Gall.

But the hooded man wasn't done. "I have the Aether Rose on board, as well as your friends. I've come to take you home."

"Where is my father?" Barthian asked. He was surprised by how brittle his voice sounded.

"My friends tell me he's somewhere on the Isle, hiding from Grimm. I don't know more than that."

Gall laughed. "See, boy? All lies. He doesn't even know!"

But Barthian had heard enough to be convinced. The gauntlet was still on his wrist, and he leveled it at Wormwood. The pirate's eyes widened, and he ordered the automaton holding Barthian to release him. The automaton obeyed and backed away.

"Oh, bother!" said Gall. "I knew I'd forgotten something!"

Wormwood laid his pistol on the deck and Barthian made his way to the skiff, keeping his gauntlet aimed at Wormwood as he threw his sack onto the deck. The hooded man, meanwhile, kept his pistols aimed at both pirates. Barthian climbed aboard.

"Release the grapple irons," the hooded man said to Barthian.

Barthian tried, but they were stuck fast on the hull of the skiff. He yanked and kicked and tried to lift the hooks from the side of the boat, but they wouldn't shift, not for Barthian anyway.

"Let me," said the hooded man, and he gave Barthian his pistols.

Barthian didn't even have time to adjust his grip on the handles before Wormwood dove at him.

Barthian dodged, and Wormwood fell forward onto the deck, scooping up his pistol and taking a quick shot at the hooded man. But the shot missed and hit the hull of *The Lamentation*, which gave Barthian and the hooded man enough time to crouch low behind the gunwale, as *The Lamentation*'s automatons opened fire simultaneously, raining a volley of bullets on the Emperor's skiff.

"We're trapped!" shouted Barthian, not daring to lift his head.

"Yes!" said the hooded man, who was looking up at the turrets of *The Lamentation*. "What's the range on that gauntlet of yours?"

"The gauntlet? I don't know."

"Let's test it. Fire up at that oil cannon on the side of that turret."

Keeping as low behind the hull as he could, Barthian aimed where the hooded man had pointed, and fired. The gauntlet's blue lightning flashed upwards and hit the cannon's mount on the side of the turret. The explosion was far beyond what Barthian would have suspected, and it rained oily fire down up the lower sections of the ship. This was all the distraction the hooded man had needed, and while the automatons on the deck momentarily ceased firing to marvel up at the oil fires that had broken out down the side of the ship, the hooded man took up a new position in the bow of the skiff and began shooting the automatons down.

Barthian couldn't believe the speed and accuracy with which he picked off his targets. Wormwood and Gall both scrambled for cover as their crew fell or burst into bits around them.

"Take over!" the hooded man shouted, and Barthian began firing his weapon around the deck, blasting automatons, blasting sections of boat, missing everything completely. It didn't matter. The lightning cracked and spat around the pirate ship and kept everyone down.

Meanwhile, the hooded man freed the skiff from the grapple irons of *The Lamentation* and told Barthian to stay at the gunwale firing at the pirate ship, while he ran to the wheelhouse to pull the skiff away. As the skiff powered up and moved towards open sky, Barthian ceased firing, while Wormwood ran to the bow and glared out over the edge, pointing his finger at Barthian.

"I will hunt you down, boy!" Barthian heard him scream. "Today, you made an enemy!"

"Two enemies actually, Wormwood!" the captain shouted, emerging beside Gall at the gunwale of The Lamentation.

"Two enemies!" Wormwood shouted, as Barthian escaped. "Today, you made two enemies!"

The Emperor's skiff was small and sleek, and the hooded man manoeuvred it easily beneath the pirate ship, out of sight of the pirates. It pulled away into the clouds, powering quickly towards No Man's Landing. As soon as Barthian was sure they were out of range of *The Lamentation*'s oil and fire cannons, he joined the hooded man in the wheelhouse ... where Salmon, Nelly, Click-Clack, and a small, aether-powered mechanical bird the size and shape of a song thrush, were waiting to greet him.

"You're here!" Barthian felt his knees go weak with relief.

"It turns out we were wrong about the man in black!" said Salmon.

"You're certainly not the first," the hooded man said. "I'm not sure why, but people always assume I'm out to do them harm!"

"I wonder why!" Salmon said.

The man in black had kept his hood over his head and the mask over his face. Even so, Barthian could see that his eyes were kind, if a little intense.

"Who are you?" Barthian asked, finally voicing the question that had been on his mind since they first saw their hooded pursuer on the hills above Heron's Rush.

"It's best you don't know," he answered. "Just trust that I'm on your side. And that I'll never be far away."

"What side would that be?" said Salmon.

"The side that's against the Usurper and everything he's done to this world."

"Mom says never trust a stranger," said Nelly.

"Your mom sounds like a very smart lady," he answered.

"So why should we trust you?"

"You don't have to trust me," he said, manoeuvring the skiff through the clouds. "But you should always trust three things."

"What are they?" said Salmon, suspiciously.

The hooded man cleared his throat. "First, trust the stories about old Aethasia, about how good it was. Because it really was very good, which tells you something about the Great Engineer."

"That makes sense," said Salmon. "We can trust that."

"Second?" Nelly asked.

"Trust kindness. When people do good things for each other, wonderful things happen. Things you could never have imagined. You can trust that."

"Sounds fair," said Nelly. "What's the last one?"

"Trust that what you build for the future is worth it."

"The future?" Salmon said.

"Yes, the future of Aethasia. You can trust that Aethasia won't be this way forever, that the Emperor won't always rule Evercity, and that people won't always be hungry and poor. Everything you do that brings the future one step closer…well, you can trust that."

"How do you know all these things?" Nelly asked.

"Because he's the Great Engineer!" Barthian said. He was surprised by how excited he felt in his chest as he said the words. But the hooded man laughed.

"No, I'm not the Great Engineer," he said. "But I do know him."

"You mean he's alive?" said Salmon.

"Of course he's alive!" said the hooded man, as if that was something everyone should know. "At least he was the last time I saw him."

"You saw him?!" Nelly asked, staring at Salmon and Barthian as if to see whether they'd heard what she'd just heard.

"Yes, of course I saw him."

"Where is he?" Barthian asked. "I need to find him."

"Oh, I can't tell you that, not yet anyway," the hooded man said. "But he's close. And he's watching. And he's on your side."

CHAPTER FOURTEEN

THE HOODED MAN brought the Emperor's skiff down in the hills outside
No Man's Landing, out beyond the back of the town where it was less
likely anyone would notice the imperial transport dirigible making an
unscheduled landing. The light was failing, marking the end of another
eventful, dramatic day, but there was much to do before Barthian could
rest that night.

"Will you not come?" Barthian asked the hooded man, as he prepared to take off again. The man had yet to remove his face mask or
volunteer his name, so none of them knew who he was. Not that it
mattered much—he had saved them all from a terrible fate, and that's
all they needed to know.

"I have to go," he said, in response to Barthian. "I have...business."

"But my father..." Barthian started. But he realised the hooded
man wouldn't change his mind.

"You will find a way. You have friends," said the hooded man,
looking to Salmon and Nelly. "Remember everything I've told you.
The Great Engineer is always close. And you can take the Techno Mite.
He will be very useful."

"Click-Clack?"

"I can't take him back to the Manor, not yet. He may as well stay
with you."

Click-Clack tilted his head to one side as though deep in thought.

"Is that such a bad thing, Click-Clack?" Barthian asked.

"Warming to the idea, bzzt!" answered the automaton. "But the bird cannot stay, bzzt!"

As the skiff lifted from the hillside, with both the hooded man and the mechanical song thrush on board, Barthian, Salmon, Nelly, and now Click-Clack, watched it go, then trudged down the hills towards No Man's Landing. Barthian told his friends how he'd been captured in the forest on the verge of taking an Aether Rose from the glade, and Nelly told Barthian how the hooded man led them through a path across the Boomlands and into the very heart of the Giant Seed Forest, where they stole the Emperor's skiff from the Echo Factory.

"Who is he, do you think?" Salmon asked.

"He knows my father, but that's all I know."

"How about you, Click-Clack?" Nelly asked. "Do you know who the hooded man is?"

But Click-Clack remained uncharacteristically quiet.

On the outskirts of the business district they bid their farewells, but there was no time for tears. Not yet anyway. Salmon and Nelly wandered away together, back towards the Grotto, while Barthian, with Click-Clack hard on his heels, made his way cautiously through the narrow, cobbled streets, making sure to avoid the patrols. There was still a price on his head, after all, and he could only assume the streets were full of spies hoping to cash in on his capture.

But there were few automaton patrols in the streets that day—just the odd Bombardier, which Barthian could avoid easily enough. As he approached the workshop for the first time in days, he paused for some time, hiding in an alleyway and watching from the shadows to try and catch the watchers out. But he saw nothing, at least nothing out of the ordinary, so he quickly darted into the workshop that he had called home for so long.

How different it looked now, with its bashed-in front door and a floor covered in broken timepieces. Even Click-Clack let out a long, low moan at the sight of the mess.

"Click-Clack repair?" the Techno-Mite asked.

"There's too much and it will take you too long," Barthian said.

"Ooooh!" said Click-Clack.

There was no sign of Barthian's father, just the evidence of Grimm's anger. Nothing in the workshop had been left intact. On top of that, it was clear that looters had been in and taken what they could find for spare parts, or what they thought were valuable little treasures and souvenirs.

Barthian couldn't blame the people of No Man's Landing for coming to see what they could find. Salvage was the town's main income now that the Emperor had all but destroyed its fishing and trading. But it was more than the mess and the looting that distressed Barthian. It was the realisation a livelihood had been destroyed. And more than that, Grimm had wrecked so many beautiful timepieces, each one with a story and a history all of its own. How would Barthian ever compensate Germain's customers for what had happened to their precious heirlooms?

Barthian didn't stay long in the workshop—it was too sad and too dangerous. He threw his sack onto Germain's bed—the looters would have cleaned out everything of value already and probably wouldn't be back—and then scurried through the streets to Lukas' warehouse, with Click-Clack stumping right behind. Thankfully, Lukas was still there, packing crates and preparing for a move. He roared with laughter to see Barthian, who quickly told him the story of the past few days: of Amos Cleverley, who turned out not to be Amos Cleverley at all, but an impostor who kidnapped them; of Mill Stone and the Whipper-Snapper automatons powered by old tech; of the Everbright Manor and how Barthian remembered being there as a small child; of the hooded man, and the Boomlands, the Giant Seed Forest, and the pirates, Wormwood and Gall.

"Well, that's some journey you've had!" said Lukas. He sounded breathless just listening to the story. "I never would have encouraged you to go, had I known you'd be in so much danger," he said, laying a hand on Barthian's shoulder.

"Then I never would have discovered so many things," Barthian said.

"I know, laddie, but still…listening to your story I realise Aethasia has become much darker than I thought."

"This came in handy," said Barthian, showing Lukas the gauntlet.

"That's for certain! Keep it for now, laddie, I've a feeling you're going to need it more than me."

Lukas was fascinated with the Techno Mite, especially the aether boiler on its back.

"I haven't seen anything like this in so long," he said. "Where did you find it again?"

"The Everbright Manor," Barthian said. "The strange thing is, I remember it, from my childhood. It must have been there for years. But father has never mentioned the Manor to me."

Lukas knelt down in front of the automaton, examining its glowing bright purple eyes.

"Click-Clack, aye?" he said.

"Affirmative. Click-Clack!" The automaton raised its small arm and pointed to Lukas's chest. "Lukas—inventor."

Lukas laughed loudly. "People call me many names, Click-Clack, most of them unpleasant! But I'll take inventor any day of the week.'"

Click-Clack made a purring sound, which Barthian interpreted as a chuckle.

"You're moving!" Barthian said then, looking around at the crates. "Why?"

"It's time, laddie. I've been marked by Grimm, and possibly by the Emperor too. I found his favour for a while, not that I wanted it. But I fear things will change. Aethasia is at a crossroads."

"Where will you go?"

"I have some options," Lukas muttered as he turned Click-Clack around, looking at all sides of him. "But mark my words, it'll be a secret place. Well away from prying eyes."

Barthian had much more to ask Lukas, but time was short, so his questions would have to go unanswered, at least for the time being. He gave Lukas the Aether Rose that the hooded man had fetched from the forest and urged him to make Germain's tonic as soon as he was able.

"I'll do it this evening, laddie, I give you my word," Lukas said. "It will need to sit overnight but will be ready by the morning."

"The other problem is…I don't where my father is hiding."

"We don't rightly know either, laddie," said Lukas. "I've passed word around my networks, but no one's heard anything."

"The hooded man said father had escaped from the mines."

"That much is true. The whole town is talking about it. Grimm is furious with your father for making him look like a fool and has pulled most of the patrols out of No Man's Landing to look for him along the cliffs. We've heard the Emperor himself is not pleased at all."

"The Emperor?"

"Aye, this has gone to the very top."

"Where could father be?"

Lukas shook his head and looked perplexed. "If he escaped from the mines, there's only one place he would have gone, unless he's injured somewhere along the way."

"Tell me!" Barthian urged.

"The hidden cave in Smugglers Cove."

"I know the one! The Pool of Stars! We were there the same night father collapsed! But I don't understand."

"There's a tunnel behind the waterfall, laddie … a tunnel that burrows below the ocean through the rocky causeway all the way to the Isle. Who made it, no one knows. But it's been there since before the days of the smugglers."

"Did Father know about it?"

"There isn't much that happens in Aethasia that your father doesn't know—you should know that by now."

"I have to go there."

"Don't bother, laddie, we've checked. He's not there. But…"

Barthian waited.

"If he fell in the tunnel, or if he was too weak to come all the way through… We can't know unless someone goes down there."

"Into the tunnel?"

"Aye. Into the tunnel."

Barthian took a big sigh. "I can't," he said, thinking of the tunnel of his nightmares.

Click-Clack came closer and made a soothing sound, like the opening notes of a gentle tune.

"He's saying you're not alone, laddie," Lukas said.

"Affirmative," said Click-Clack. "Not alone, bzzt. Click-Clack. Salmon. Nelly."

"I can't ask any more of them," Barthian said. It would be easier for him to walk alone through a tunnel all the way out to the Isle, than to drag his friends into more danger.

"Ah, laddie, you still don't get it!" Lukas said.

Barthian frowned. "What don't I get?"

"Have you never been told about the secret properties of aether, about why it was such a powerful source of energy in the Great Engineer's old tech?"

"I know hardly anything about it," he said, "other than what I've seen with my own eyes."

"Aether generates its own power," said Lukas. "Perpetual energy. It's like it's alive. Fogrock is different. Fogrock burns out, so you need more and more of it. But aether... aether is... everlasting."

Barthian remembered what Salmon had said about the crystals at the Aether Swell, about how there was something living in them.

"I don't understand it either," Lukas admitted. "But what I do know is that aether is most powerful around friendship. Love. Kindness. Selflessness. Things like that are what Aethasia was built on, and they're the things the Emperor hated more than anything. He wouldn't rest until aether was eradicated from the land, and until the Great Engineer had fled in shame. But no one can destroy such a thing, laddie. Not when it feeds off the things that all Aethasians, deep in their hearts, truly want."

"You could outlaw friendship," said Barthian. "That would do it."

Lukas laughed. "There's a wise thinker in you, laddie. That's the very reason the Emperor is determined to make Aethasia such a hateful, suspicious place. Friendship and love are the enemy, as much as aether or the Great Engineer. But he will never eradicate it, not all of it. Not while there's people like you left in Aethasia."

Click-Clack rocked back and forward on the heels of his metal boots.

"You need your friends, laddie," Lukas said. "Not because they're useful, or because you don't want to be alone. You need your friends, because without them you will never truly experience Aethasia. You owe it to yourself to discover just how special this land used to be."

Barthian took a deepbreath. He knew deep inside that Lukas was speaking truthfully and wisely. He let out another big sigh, then patted the top of Click-Clack's head.

"Come on, little Techno Mite," Barthian said. "We need to visit some friends in the Grotto."

⁓

Salmon didn't need to be asked twice. Of course he would go with Barthian to the Isle. But Nelly had another mission in mind.

"I'm going to find help," she said.

"There isn't time," argued Salmon.

"We can't do this alone," she said. "We need more friends for this."

"We're going to have to crawl through a tight, tiny tunnel underneath the sea," Barthian said, already feeling cold at the mere thought of living his nightmare.

"We've been through worse things already," Nelly reassured him, touching his arm.

"Anyway, things are easier when friends have your back," said Salmon, winking at Nelly.

"You both sound like Lukas," Barthian said.

"Just as long as I don't look like Lukas!" Salmon said.

They set off the next morning, Barthian and Salmon heading in one direction and Nelly in another—to where, exactly, she wouldn't say. Barthian had wrapped Lukas' tonic in a cloth for protection just as soon as it was ready and put it in his pocket, right beside Grimm's watch, where it would be safe. Then he joined his friends in the Grotto, and from there they made their way down to the coves, following the path Barthian and his father had walked together so many times. For once, Smugglers Cove was deserted—not even the Combustonaut that usually guarded the beach and the entrance to the secret cave could be seen.

"Lukas said all the patrols had been called in to look for my father," Barthian said.

"Maybe so," said Salmon, "but keep your eyes open. I don't like the feel of this."

Barthian lifted the loose planking on the entrance to the cave and Salmon led the way in, followed by Click-Clack. Barthian joined them, and felt the nerves rising up inside him again as he entered the narrow tunnel that led through to the Pool of Stars.

"This is my new favourite place!" said Salmon, as they regrouped around the pool.

"Affirmative, bzzt!" said Click-Clack.

Barthian had other things on his mind, like finding the tunnel. The waterfall flowed from above and streamed into the Pool of Stars, and in all their years of coming to the cave, Barthian had never seen his father pay it any attention. Barthian leaned against the wall of the cave beside the tumbling water and peered behind the stream, and there it was, the mouth of a tunnel. Not quite as small as he had feared, but certainly small enough that they would have to crouch as they walked—apart from Click-Clack, of course.

Click-Clack went into the tunnel first, because his bright eyes could illuminate the darkness for Barthian and the others. He walked fearlessly through the water and out into the hole in the rock face.

"Well, here goes," said Barthian, steeling himself. He followed Click-Clack through the waterfall, crouching so that he wouldn't bang his head against the roof of the tunnel, then found himself immediately in the darkness behind the Techno Mite, who was treading carefully because the tunnel headed downwards at a steep angle. His aether-powered eyes shone brightly, and the aether boiler on his back was nice and bright too.

Salmon entered the tunnel next.

"Whoa, steep!" he said, almost slipping on the wet rock. "Glad you're at the head of the pack, Click-Clack!"

"Bzzt!" said Click-Clack, but for once he didn't sound so happy.

Onwards he went, though, and so did the rest, walking slowly with their backs hunched over, following the light of the aether boiler in front of them. Barthian couldn't help noticing that the light seemed to calm him and give him extra strength, of both character and will.

Good. He needed it. This tunnel looked so similar to the tunnel of his nightmares that he was having difficulty separating the two. He had to remind himself that the nightmare wasn't real, and that here, in this tunnel, he was with friends, and the goal was the most important thing to him: reaching his father and bringing him back to safety.

Eventually, the tunnel leveled off and headed straight towards the Isle. It opened up as well, so that they could stand almost fully upright. Click-Clack continued to stump on ahead of them, oblivious to fear or discomfort. This was what he was designed to do, support others in their mission. The whole time, Barthian peered ahead to where the soft, purple light illuminated the rocky floor, watching for signs of his father. But there was nothing, and Barthian was conflicted about it. On the one hand, it meant that his father hadn't fallen in the tunnel as Lukas had suggested, but on the other, it meant that they would have to walk all the way to the Isle, and the thought of that made Barthian uneasy.

It took what felt like an age. The Isle was a good distance out in the bay from the docks at No Man's Landing, too far to swim, and almost too far to make the journey by row boat. The mine bulkers did the trip in no time, because they had to—Aethasia had become greedy for fogrock which is why the mines, the miners, and the bulkers all worked around the clock. Barthian heard the bulker passing overhead at one point, its big propellers churning up the ocean above the tunnel as it steamed towards the Isle for another load of fogrock. Eventually though, Barthian saw what appeared to be the first sign of natural light, a faint glimmer way ahead. The tunnel was climbing again, not as steeply as it did from the cave, but in a gradual incline that made all of them, except Click-Clack, puffed out. The more they climbed the brighter the light became, until Barthian had no doubt at all that he was seeing the exit onto the Isle.

"Wait, Click-Clack!" Barthian said, when they were less than fifty feet from the opening. "Let me go ahead."

Click-Clack pressed up against the wall of the tunnel while Barthian squeezed through to take the lead.

"I need to see what's out there before we go charging out!"

Barthian crept ahead, his gauntlet raised towards the mouth of the tunnel. As he got closer he saw that the opening was concealed from the other side by vegetation—vines and shrubs growing from the sand around the rock, which explained how the tunnel had never been discovered by Grimm and his automatons. At the mouth of the tunnel itself, Barthian began to crawl, then at the very edge he lay on his belly and edged forward, trying to peek through the vines at the scene outside the tunnel.

It was a small glade, not unlike Smuggler's Cove, except smaller and more lush, with trees and exotic plants, thick green bushes, and a small beach with sparkling white sand—not the picture he had ever had of the Isle, which everyone described as gloomy and dark and fog-ridden. But the cove was a reminder of how the Isle used to be, back before the Emperor made it a place of industry and punishment.

Barthian crept further forward, and saw an overgrown path from the tunnel down to the beach, hugging the cliff face to his right. Smoke rose from the beach where the ocean lapped onto the sand, and when Barthian raised himself onto his hands and knees he saw a figure, dressed in a tatty hooded cape, sitting cross-legged beside a little fire, on which he was baking fish while he gazed out across the sea.

"Father!" Barthian whispered, not daring to shout in case it wasn't his father at all. The hood covered the man's face and hair, and despite how much the figure resembled his father he couldn't be entirely sure.

Salmon crept up beside Barthian, who stood with his gauntlet raised while Click-Clack stayed behind.

"Who is it?" Salmon whispered.

"I can't tell," Barthian said. "But it looks like my father."

"The coast looks clear," said Salmon, trying to get a better look at the cliff top and the trees around the glade. "There's only one way to find out." Salmon began to head out, but Barthian held him back.

"No, I have to," he said. "Stay here!"

Barthian emerged from the tunnel, quietly pushing through the vines and creeping behind the bushes onto the goat trail. He followed it down to the beach, looking around him the whole time, his gauntlet raised, ready for trouble. Then he stepped quietly over the sand towards the figure at the water's edge. He got within three feet without making a sound, and then whispered, "Father?"

The figure turned, surprised, but the hood still shielded his face. So Barthian ripped it off quickly, and there was his father at last, but with a gag around his mouth and his hands tied together on his lap. His eyes shone with warmth at Barthian, but immediately widened in horror—automatons emerging from every hiding place around the glade, their weapons raised at father and son, even as Barthian spun around with his gauntlet ready to fire.

"That would be very foolish!" said an icy cold voice, as Grimm stepped out from a cleft in the rock face, his exoskeleton huffing and hissing out fog as he strode forward across the sand.

Barthian didn't back down. He kept his gauntlet trained on Grimm, and his fingers on the palm trigger. But all around the glade, automatons continued to emerge. And there on the goat trail were Salmon and Click-Clack, being dragged down towards the beach by heavily-weaponised Pacifiers.

"You think I don't know every inch of this miserable island?" Grimm asked.

"I knew the moment the hooded stranger let you off the Emperor's stolen skiff that you would try an assault on the Isle mines," Grimm continued. "We'd captured your dreary father in no time at all. He can barely breathe, so he could hardly crawl on all fours back to the mainland."

Barthian leant down and took the gag from his father's mouth, and his father took a big breath.

"Thank you, son!" he said, quietly, and the warmth slowly returned to his eyes.

Salmon and Click-Clack joined them, as Barthian took the bonds from his father's wrists. Then he helped him stand and they stood holding one another as the automatons closed in.

"Rats, all of you!" said Grimm.

"Not rats—friends," Barthian said.

Click-Clack's eyes glowed brighter than ever, because up near the opening of the tunnel came a cry, followed by a sudden charge of urchins down the goat trail, lots of them, led by Nelly and Benny the fog catcher, wielding sticks and bricks and catapult gauntlets and fire gauntlets and canes and old rusty rifles. Some of them even carried the sails they had used to catch the fog up on the hills west of No Man's Landing when Barthian first met them. They rushed onto the beach and attacked the automatons with a ferocity that surprised even Barthian. They ran wildly around the glade, weaving between the hapless automatons as they knocked off heads, buckled their limbs, set Troubleshooters alight, smashed fog boilers, and caught automatons large and small in their nets.

"Noooo!" screamed Grimm, who charged at Barthian, knocking him to the sand. But Grimm hadn't accounted for Click-Clack, who put his head down and ran at the Overseer, catching him full in the belly. Grimm fell backwards onto the sand and Barthian, quick as a flash of lightning from his gauntlet, was back on his feet and standing over him, pointing the weapon at Grimm's chest.

"Salmon!" he shouted. "Cut down the vines so we can tie him up!"

Salmon scurried off through the melee that continued around the cove, but even though the battle continued it was clear that the automatons were overwhelmed and defeated, as the urchins outwitted, outran, and outsmarted Grimm's forces.

"You will pay for this," Grimm sneered. "There is no place in Aethasia that you can go where I will not pursue you."

"I wouldn't be so sure about that," said Germain. "What time is it, Barty?"

Barthian reached into his pocket for Grimm's watch and felt sudden pain, both in his hand and in the leg the pocket was against. The pocket was all wet, and Barthian realised the fall had broken the vial of tonic that Lukas had made for his father, cutting into his leg. He took out the watch anyway, and it was covered in sticky purple medicine. Germain saw what it was and knew what must have happened. He knew the implications as well. He reached out and ruffled his son's hair.

"It's time to go," Barthian said.

"Yes," said Germain. "Yes, it is."

They left Grimm on the beach, tied up in vines and surrounded by the broken and incapacitated figures of his automatons, still burning, twitching, or wandering around headless, limbless, and totally aimless. As Barthian and Germain led the urchins into the tunnel, with Click-Clack ahead of them illuminating the way once more, they heard Grimm shouting for help. But no one was coming. His automatons would find him in a day or so…but not today.

It was a slow and steady journey back to the Pool of Stars. Germain was weak and weary, and the cold, damp air of the tunnel tormented his chest. But on and on they stumbled, and as they approached the steep incline of the last section up into the cave, Germain held onto Click-Clack, who pulled him slowly up into the light. Germain took step after step after step, back to whatever freedom they had in No Man's Landing. And in the cave Germain finally collapsed, and lay beside the pool with his burning hot face almost touching the water.

"He's dying," Barthian said to Nelly and Salmon, as their urchin friends filed past them through the cave and out into Smuggler's Cove.

Nelly put her hand on Barthian's arm. "What can we do?"

"He needs more tonic," Salmon said.

"No!" Germain said, sweat glistening on his brow. "No more."

He gestured to Barthian to come close, and Barthian knelt down and brought his face near to his father's.

"The Old Mount!" Germain said.

"I don't understand."

"The Old Mount. I want to go to the Old Mount."

"It's a day's walk away, father," Barthian said. "You'll never make it."

"Old Quinby Crabb," Germain whispered.

"The fishmonger?"

"Yes!" Germain said, nodding. "Quinby Crabb. Has a cart. And a horse."

"You don't want me to steal Quinby Crabb's horse and cart!"

"No, no…he owes me. From a long time ago. He'll remember. Tell him why you need it."

"I'll go," Salmon said. "I'll get the cart. You stay with your father."

Nelly went with Salmon while Barthian and Click-Clack stayed with Germain in the cave, looking up at the sky and longing for more of these times but realising this was probably the last…unless something magical could be done.

"You need tonic," Barthian said to Germain. "The tonic will make you better."

Germain shook his head again. "It's gone too far," he said, tapping his chest. "It's too late. Just one last thing…"

"What?" said Barthian, who would do absolutely anything if it meant keeping his father alive. "What can I do?"

Germain brought him close again. "The Great Engineer!"

"The Great—! Father, you're delirious!"

"No, son," Germain insisted. "We need to go to the Old Mount… find the Engineer."

Germain closed his eyes and fell into a feverish sleep. Barthian collected fresh water from the waterfall and and wiped it across his brow.

"Click-Clack help?" Click-Clack asked.

Barthian wiped a hand across his eyes and sniffed. "There's nothing you can do, Click-Clack."

Nothing that mattered, anyway. But Click-Clack kept asking for something to do, so when Salmon and Nelly returned and said they had fetched the cart to the entrance to Smugglers Cove, Barthian sent Click-Clack back to take care of the workshop, just to get him out of the way.

"There isn't much left in there that's of any value," he told the automaton. "Just my sack, and the scarlet cloak I found in the Manor. Oh, and you might fix the front door and tidy up the place while I'm away. I expect we'll be back in a day or so. Hopefully Father will be ready to work again."

Salmon and Nelly helped Barthian lift his father onto the cart, where he lay down in the back beside a small barrel of fresh water that Salmon had placed there for the journey, as Barthian hopped in front and took the reins. Then they bid their farewells, which were tearful this time, and they all knew that one way or another, the next time they met things would be very different indeed.

"Take care of yourself," Nelly said. She climbed up on the cart and kissed his cheek.

"You take care of each other," Barthian said, blushing. "Grimm may come after you."

"No chance!" Salmon said. "Like I always say, it's you he wants." Salmon climbed up on the cart and gave Barthian what he called an urchin wrap. "Once we urchins grab onto something, we never let go!" he explained.

"Okay, okay!" said Barthian, shaking him off playfully. "I get the meaning!"

As Salmon hopped down again he caught sight of the sign on the side of the cart, and the name that was etched in the wood.

"Would you look at that!" he said. "Everbright & Sons."

"That's funny," said Nelly. "You hear a name once, then suddenly you see it everywhere!"

"Huh!" said Barthian, leaning over to look at the name. "That's a strange coincidence. I wonder why the fishmonger has an Everbright cart?"

The question could wait until he returned. If he was to make the Old Mount by nightfall he needed to be on his way. As Nelly waved, and as Click-Clack let out a mournful noise, Barthian set off—toward what end he had no idea. At best there was a slim hope that Germain knew something no one else did, and that there was a magical cure waiting for him somewhere on the Old Mount. At worst, this was a fool's errand created by a feverish mind.

It was early afternoon and heavy, grey clouds filled the sky and threatened rain, which started to fall before the afternoon was done. The fishmonger had put canopies in the cart that he used as awnings over his stall, and Barthian stopped to drag them across the cart to shield himself and Germain from the worst of the storm. With the canopy over his head, Barthian set his sights on the Old Mount and persisted against the wind and the rain.

"Please be out there!" he said out loud, though he could barely hear the sound of his own voice against the rain hitting the canopy over his head. "If you're still alive, please be out there!"

But Barthian wasn't even sure who he was saying it to.

CHAPTER FIFTEEN

BY THE TIME they reached the foot of the mountain the rain had stopped, but the clouds sat heavily over the peak. The road up the side of the Old Mount was a steep track over jumbled stone that wrapped around the skirts of the mountain like a decorative tree. Even at the foot of the mountain Barthian could see the entire landscape to the sea, with No Man's Landing in the near distance. On a clearer day he would have been able to see the Fogworks belching out its smoke over in the east, but the mists had already risen from the wastelands and were sweeping quickly across Aethasia.

Barthian stopped to adjust the canopy and check on Germain. He was still sleeping and the fever had dropped, which gave Barthian some hope. He looked around for signs of a patrol but didn't expect to confront any automatons on the Old Mount. He could never be too certain, though. He set off again, as the horse pulled the cart farther and farther up and around, past copses of trees prevailing against the winds that swept down from the peak, and over bridges that crossed chasms and mountain streams.

As they got higher, the vegetation thinned out, and the mountainside resembled the scrub that lay across the moors out to the west of No Man's Landing. The mountainside was sparse where the plants and the trees were powerless against the high winds, but the heather that lay round about had a charm of its own. There were birds, too, from the smallest sparrows pecking at the scrub, to great eagles he could see soaring up near the clouds, and hawks that sat in the sky as if perched on invisible ledges, before diving steep and fast to catch some mouse or rabbit or mountain hen.

After the scrub came the snow, which appeared suddenly and unexpectedly, as if it was a rug that someone had unfurled from the top of the mountain. It lay thick on the ground and Barthian felt the drop in the temperature as rapidly as the hawk had fallen from the sky. He brought the canopy back over Germain and himself, not because the rain was falling but to keep the cold at bay. Even so, he spent the rest of the journey shivering and rubbing his arms so that they wouldn't freeze. He checked Germain and realised that despite the cold he was as hot as he had been beside the Pool of Stars. The fever wasn't letting go.

"Time is critical, father," he said, placing his hand on his father's brow.

"Ugh," Germain moaned, and tried to open his eyes.

"Rest, father," Barthian said, his heart breaking. "We're almost there."

He looked around them at the snowscape and peered up towards where the mountain vanished into the clouds, but there was still no sign of a Great Engineer. For that matter, there was no sign of anyone.

"I just wish I knew where 'there' was," he said to himself, before geeing the horse on its way yet again.

Around the next pass the road took a turn, and instead of winding round the Old Mount it began to wind upwards, with sharper bends and a steeper climb. Barthian began to fear that the horse wouldn't make it, and perhaps the horse was suspecting that too, because it hesitated as Barthian snapped the reins. But it pressed on and climbed higher, and just before they reached the clouds they came across an old camp.

Barthian dismounted to have a closer look, and to give the horse a rest. He found old water pots and evidence of a fire, and the remains of a little hut that someone had built from sticks that they must have brought up from the lower reaches of the mountain. It wasn't much, but it was the only sign of life he had seen since setting off from the base, and it gave just a glimmer—the faintest glimmer—of hope that they weren't alone, and that sooner or later they would come across someone, anyone, who could point them in the right direction.

"Barthian!" Germain shouted from the cart, and Barthian jumped with fright. He rushed to his father, who was trying to lift himself up.

"No father, rest," Barthian said, but Germain persisted.

"No, no." Germain gave his head an exaggerated shake, groping for the sides of the wagon to pull himself up. "We need to talk...time is running out."

"We have plenty of time, father," Barthian said, trying to ease Germain and make him lie down again. "We're almost at the summit, I can feel it."

"No, we won't make it. Talk now." He gripped Barthian by the arm, so hard it hurt. "Talk now!"

Barthian adjusted the canopy again, and they sat together in the back of the cart, sheltered from the elements as best they could be. Germain took Barthian's hand and held it firmly as if his son was about to escape. But Barthian was going nowhere.

"I need to tell you things," Germain began. "While I can."

He hung his head and Barthian thought he'd fallen unconscious, but then he began to speak.

"I was the Great Engineer's apprentice," Germain began. "Long ago. Apprentice to the master timekeeper. But I made a terrible error of judgment—" Germain coughed, and coughed again.

"Father, please, we must keep moving."

"No, Barty, this is important. You need to hear."

"Speak slowly then. Keep your breath steady."

"I made a mistake," Germain said, still rushing, eager to finish his story. "I supported the Usurper...thought the Great Engineer was finished...and his use of aether misguided and weak..."

Germain hung his head again. "The Great Engineer knew that I had betrayed him...he fled Aethasia, never knowing that I was sorry. He must have despised me..."

Barthian placed his arm on his father's back.

"I realised my mistake...and I denounced the Emperor. I wasn't the only one. Others from the court in Evercity realised their error…we all ended up in the Fogworks…"

"Father, I'm so sorry."

"I'm dying today because of that miserable place. But I don't regret my time there…not one bit."

Barthian sat back in shock. "How can you say that, father?"

But Germain continued as if he hadn't heard. "There was a young couple in the Fogworks…they had been in the court as well, for a time. We became friends. They had done some terrible things…but they fell out of favour with the Emperor. They had a child…he was born before they were captured and thrown in the Fogworks. Cassandra, the Overseer, she hated the child…he was so smart, so cheeky. She threatened to kill the boy. One day she took the child and held him close to the furnace…but then relented and gave the child back. But…but the couple knew she would come again. And so…"

Barthian didn't want the gears to fit together this way, the way he somehow knew they were going to fit… "Father?"

"They gave their boy to me…I had been planning my escape…me and Quinby Crabb. We had been digging a tunnel…so we escaped…and I took the child as my own…"

Barthian was silent, remembering a small tunnel, and the heat of the Fogworks, and the tight grip of his father's hand, the same hand that held him now. The tunnel of his nightmares was the tunnel his father had made to give him freedom.

"Barthian," Germain said, turning to look his son in the eyes. "I am not your father. Your parents, they never left the Fogworks. If they are alive, they are there still."

"Father, I don't—"

"Jude and Magda…they are your parents…"

Germain's eyes were vacant and his head was listing to one side. But he was fighting it, snapping himself out of whatever it was that was trying to pull him down.

"I have heard the names Jude and Magda before," Barthian said. "The boatman on the River of Bones said they…they murdered a boy at the Everbright Manor."

"They are Everbrights," Germain said. "Cousins of the Great Engineer. They betrayed him…betrayed Joshua…"

Germain's head fell forward as he collapsed from the strain. Barthian felt a great pressure building up his chest, like a wave on the ocean, building and building until it crashed on the sand. Except this wave just kept rising until Barthian thought he would choke. But there were other things to worry about now. He felt his father's head and listened to his heart, which was still beating, but faintly, and erratically. He laid Germain down and rushed to the front of the cart to grab the reins and snap the horse into action again.

The horse must have felt his urgency because it kicked away, trotting quickly up the mountain pass. On and on it rose, up into the clouds which consumed them like a ghostly white shroud that blocked Barthian's vision on all sides. He was travelling blind in more ways than one. His eyes stung with the tears that fell freely and silently, but he had to hold all that in. He had to keep going.

And then—two massive doors in the face of the mountain took shape through the mist, set against a giant bronze frame, with etchings in the frame and mouldings on the doors that reminded him of the etchings and design of the aether device on the back of the Whipper-snappers in Mill Stone.

But in front of the doors were standing three giant automaton Lashers, and they were heading towards Barthian and the wagon.

"Father, we're here!" Barthian shouted. "Here at last! But we're in trouble."

Germain stirred in the back of the cart, managing to lift his head and look out from beneath the cover at the three Lashers heading towards them.

"Barthian turn around!" he said, as forcefully as he could. "It's not worth it."

"I'm not turning around," Barthian said, defiantly. "You need to see the Great Engineer, and we're going to find him."

As the Lashers approached they flexed and snapped their long arms, which sparked with the same energy as Barthian's gauntlet. Barthian realised that one blow from a lashing arm would be near fatal. But he was determined to get around them. He leapt to the ground and took up a fighting stance, his gauntlet leveled at the lead Lasher, whose arms were unfurled by its side, ready to strike.

"If you move any closer, I'll fire!" Barthian warned, bracing his feet to steady himself.

The Lasher ignored him and kept moving forward, snapping its arms to charge them. The crack of the charge was loud and clear in the mountain air, a deafening snap that left Barthian in no doubt of how much power these automatons had. Suddenly the Lasher flicked out at Barthian, narrowly missing his head but leaving an arc of blue light and dark smoke in the air above him. It was a warning shot, but Barthian wasn't backing down. He fired his gauntlet full in the automaton's mid-carriage and for a moment it staggered as if it was about to fall.

But it didn't fall. It just swayed a little as it adjusted to the strike. Barthian fired again, and this time the Lasher barely even registered the hit. It lashed out with both arms this time, aiming for Barthian's head.

But Barthian was ready this time and dived to the ground as the Lasher's arms connected and sent sparks raining down upon him. Now Barthian was vulnerable, lying flat on his belly, with a weapon that was no match for the fearsome automaton now preparing to take a final strike. Barthian closed his eyes and covered his head with his arms, and in his mind he pictured the Great Engineer and the hooded man and—

Suddenly, his father stood above him, holding the barrel of fresh water that Salmon had placed in the back of the cart for the journey. Without a word, Germain threw the contents of the barrel over the approaching Lashers, which suddenly halted in their tracks, twitching and jerking, with smoke emerging from the units as the water caused their electrified arms to short-circuit.

"Now, Barthian!" Germain shouted.

Barthian didn't need to be told twice. Up on his feet he jumped and fired his weapon at the first Lasher, the blue flame from his gauntlet hitting the automaton in the green-glowing grille in the front of its chest. Weakened by the water, the Lasher buckled and bent, then fell over backwards and burst into flames.

Emboldened, Barthian charged forward, firing again and again at the two remaining Lashers, which tried to retreat towards the doors in the mountain. He caught the one on the right, which spun around and toppled over face first, twitching and smoking on the ground. Then Barthian chased the other to the very edge of the mountain, where it stopped and made one final attempt to hit Barthian with its electrified arms. But Barthian was too quick, crouching low and hitting the automaton in the legs, then in the head, and finally in the chest, knocking the Lasher backwards and over the side of the Old Mount, where it tumbled into the mist below.

"We did it!" Barthian shouted, spinning around to his father.

But Germain wasn't over by the cart. He was over by the great doors, having collapsed onto the ground, his head leaning forward on his chest.

"Father!" Barthian shouted, but there was no answer. Barthian ran to him and grabbed his hand, and held it tightly. But Germain's hand was cold—a different kind of cold to that which came off the snow. It was the most dreadful kind of cold of all.

Germain had gone.

⤮

Barthian sat with his back to the big doors in the mountain, with his father in his arms. The horse stood grazing at a clump of wild grass at the edge of a rocky outcrop, still harnessed to the cart. Barthian had no idea how long he had sat there. He could have checked Grimm's watch, but he despised it now, and almost threw it over the edge of the mountain. But time didn't matter anymore. The timekeeper was dead. So what if Aethasia's clocks were slowing down? Now there was no one who would discover why.

His father's final words kept flashing in his mind, but nothing coherent would stay there. It was just a jumble of images and thoughts, mysterious faces and patches of reality or fantasy, all thrown in together: I am an Everbright. My father is not my father. My parents are in the Fogworks, if they're alive at all. My father betrayed the Great Engineer. The Engineer despises my father. My parents betrayed and murdered a boy. I am an Everbright. My father betrayed my kin. My father rescued me from the Fogworks. Germain Epistlethwaite risked his life for me.

It was all too much. Barthian looked out at the mist, felt its dampness in his hair and on his skin, held his father closer, and gave not one thought to what he would do next or how he would leave this spot on the mountainside.

Barthian would have stayed there forever, maybe, or at least until he froze to death. But there was a rumbling in the mountain behind him, like great cogs beginning to turn, and he felt the doors pushing against his back. He stood and took his father beneath the arms and pulled him away from the great doors. He tried to do it gently, but Germain seemed strangely heavier without life in him, and Barthian had to scramble a bit as the doors swung outwards, ever so slowly, creaking like a giant, rusted engine that hasn't cranked over for years and years.

As the doors opened, light emerged from inside the Old Mount, bursting out into the clouds—a soft, purple light, flashing as if from jewels in a chest.

Barthian peered inside, but the tunnel sloped away out of sight. All that could be seen was light, reflecting off the roof of the tunnel that was lined with the same polished bronze as the giant pillars on either side of the great doors. Then, as Barthian waited, a group of people walked up the tunnel and emerged from the light.

They were clothed in blue and purple boiler suits and their hands were covered in grease. They had grease stains on their cheeks as well, and each one had a pair of goggles sitting on his and her head. They wore big protective boots and work belts, with tools the likes of which Barthian had never seen hanging from their waists. Without speaking, they bent down and took Germain's body, then carried it inside the halls of the mountain. Barthian followed but was stopped on the threshold by a new figure, also dressed like an engineer, with grease on her hands and her face.

"Germain will be safe with us," she said, warmly but firmly.

"Where are you taking him?" Barthian asked.

"Somewhere safe."

"Can I come too?"

"No," said the lady. "You're needed here."

"Needed?"

"Time is short," she said. "And you have a part to play."

"What part?" Barthian demanded. Could no one in all Aethasia just give simple answers? "Why is timing running out?"

She didn't answer. She simply smiled and turned to head back inside.

"Wait!" Barthian said, and she stopped. "Will you heal my father?"

The woman looked confused. "No," she said simply. "He is dead."

"But…" Barthian began, and he felt the emotion welling up in his throat. "I thought…"

"Fear not," said the lady. "Your father will be safe with us."

"Just one more thing!" said Barthian, and she smiled again. He reached inside his pocket and brought out the watch. He offered it to her, and she received it carefully, and read the inscription on the back: *To my special apprentice, G.E.*

"It is beautiful," she said.

"It belongs to the Great Engineer. He gave it to the Emperor, before the…before the Usurping. The Emperor gave it away. I thought—well, I thought the Great Engineer might want it back…if you ever see him."

"This was never the Usurper's watch," she said sharply. "This was a gift from the Great Engineer to Germain Epistlethwaite—G.E., the apprentice he loved. But it was never given. The Usurper took it for his own the day that Evercity fell."

"It was my father's watch?" Barthian said. "And he never knew?"

"It is your watch now, Barthian Everbright," the lady in the boiler suit said. "Use it well."

Then she walked away, back towards the light, and the doors began to close, leaving Barthian outside alone in the cold. When the doors slammed shut with a heavy thud that seemed to make the whole mountainside shudder, he banged on the door with his fists and kicked out with his boots. He felt the urge to look down the dark path behind him, but also feared to see what might be there—pirates or more automatons or Grimm or who knew what else? Why wouldn't they let him inside where he would be safe? How could they leave him out here anyway? Didn't they care? This wasn't fair! So many questions, and so few answers.

He kicked again and again, then put his back to the doors and slid to the ground, where he put his head in his hands and cried until he felt weak with grief. Just once, he heard noises behind him and thought that they had changed their minds and would let him in… but he was wrong.

It was no more than the inhabitants of the mountain going about their business, as if the world hadn't actually come to an end.

CHAPTER SIXTEEN

CLICK-CLACK HAD DONE such a good job of tidying up the workshop, including reassembling the smashed front door by bolting metal bands across the splintered wood. In fact when Barthian returned it was almost as if nothing of the previous few days had actually happened. Except of course that Germain was no longer there, so the workshop was quiet and sad, and was missing the warmth of his voice and his passion for timepieces.

And, of course, the workshop was missing the sound of clockwork, because Grimm's automatons had destroyed every last timepiece on the shelves. Click-Clack had picked up and swept up every last piece of broken watch and clock and put them in a wooden crate he had fetched from Lukas's warehouse. So, the place was tidy...but it was no longer home.

"We can't stay here!" Barthian said, as Click-Clack showed him what a good job he had done cleaning up his father's old room. "It's too dangerous. Grimm won't stop until he catches me and takes back the watch, which I will never let him have."

"Your intentions? Bzzt," Click-Clack asked.

Barthian knew in his heart what he wanted to do. He also knew that it wasn't possible, not yet anyway. "I don't know," he said. "Run. Hide. Settle in the hills, or the Old Mount, or across the sea? Or live under the sea!"

"Nautilina!" Click-Clack said, bouncing from one foot to the other.

"Exactly!" Barthian replied, with a chuckle. "We could go and discover Nautilina. I always doubted the place existed, but I'll believe anything after what I've discovered over the past few days."

"Everbright Manor?"

Barthian fell silent. He had lived there once, he knew that now for certain. But could he live there again, knowing that his parents—his real parents—had betrayed the Great Engineer?

"I don't know, Click-Clack," he said. "I really don't know."

Click-Clack had laid the scarlet cloak on Germain's bed, and Barthian felt the cloth between his fingertips. It was strangely comforting, a link to a happier time. He wondered whether the next stage of his life should be spent trying to recover that happy place. But he quickly realised there wasn't much chance of that now that his father was gone.

And there was still the mystery of Aethasia's clockwork to solve. Something Germain had said had troubled him all the way down the mountain: the Great Engineer was the master timekeeper. Had he designed clockwork? If so, had he designed it with a fatal flaw, one that was counting down to a cataclysmic event? If so, what was it? If so, why? So much left to answer, and the thought of finding those answers without the help of his father made Barthian feel all the more alone.

"Not alone!" said Click-Clack, as if reading Barthian's thoughts. "Salmon. Nelly. Click-Clack."

"I know, Click-Clack," Barthian said, patting the Techno Mite on the head. "I know I'm not alone. But…I'm no one now."

"You're not no one!" said a familiar voice from the doorway to the workshop, and Barthian turned to see the hooded man.

"What are you doing here?" Barthian asked.

"Oh, I'm on the run, as usual. Does Grimm never rest?"

"I don't think he does," said Barthian. "But I'm glad to hear he's after you this time."

"Oh, he's after you too, don't worry about that." The hooded man was surprisingly glib for having news like that.

Barthian took a step back. "So you led him here!?"

"He's way behind, don't worry. Anyway, I needed to talk."

"Talk about what?"

"I don't know…stuff?"

"Stuff?" Barthian fought the urge to yank on his own hair in frustration.

"What happened to all your clocks? I thought this was the time-keeper's workshop?"

Barthian hung his head. "It was. But the timekeeper's dead."

"Oh, I'm sorry to hear that! Genuinely. Click-Clack, make us a cup of tea, would you?"

"Affirmative, bzzt." Click-Clack trotted over to the pantry and started to make a clatter and a fuss.

"Unless it's any trouble…" the hooded man called to the Techno-Mite, giving Barthian a wink.

"No trouble, bzzt!"

"Look, I'm sorry, but I need to pack up and get away," Barthian asked.

"Yes, yes, don't mind me," the hooded man said, pulling up a chair for himself and getting comfortable. "So what happened to all the clocks?"

"It was Grimm," Barthian said. "He wasn't happy with us."

"Naughty, naughty. What did you do?"

"Not naughty at all," Barthian snapped. "He wanted father to fix his watch, which turns out not to be his watch at all, but my father's watch, which the Great Engineer had intended to give him."

"Oh, really?" The hooded man's eyebrows went up. "Did he smash that too?"

"No, I have it here," said Barthian, and pulled out the watch and held it in his palm for the hooded man to see.

"That's beautiful," he said, looking closely at the face. "Aether crystal…very nicely done. But…" he said, taking another look, then glancing outside at the light.

"But what?"

"That's not the right time. The watch is running slow!"

"That's what Grimm wanted us to fix."

"So why didn't you?"

"Because the problem wasn't the watch, the problem was... clockwork."

"Clockwork?"

"Every timepiece in Aethasia is wrong. They're all slowing down, like they were designed with a flaw."

Barthian couldn't see the hooded man's face behind the mask and the goggles, but the man was at least silent for a while after hearing that.

"Tell me more," he said, finally.

"There's nothing more to tell," answered Barthian. "I haven't been able to solve it yet, and now the timekeeper has gone."

"No, he hasn't," the hooded man said.

"He has!" said Barthian. "I was there when he went."

"You were the apprentice to the timekeeper, correct?"

"Yes."

"When the timekeeper goes, his apprentice is the timekeeper."

"I'm no timekeeper."

"That's not what I've heard."

"What have you heard?" Where in Aethasia did this person get his information?

"I've heard you're not the son of the timekeeper at all. You're an Everbright!"

Barthian narrowed his eyes. "Who told you that?"

"Doesn't matter! Is it true?"

Click-Clack handed the hooded man a cup of tea.

"Thank you ... you haven't lost your touch! Well," he said, back to Barthian, "is it?"

"Apparently so." Maybe that would make the man stop talking about it. Barthian didn't want to think about not being Germain's son.

The hooded man straightened and held his hands out to his sides. "Then, you're an apprentice no more. Get to it!" He lifted the teacup delicately to his lips and took a sip.

"But I'm only fourteen years old."

"A lot can change when you think you're only a child. Take it from me! Anyway, there's no flaw in Aethasia's clockwork."

"How do you know?"

"Because this is a sign," the hooded man said, holding up the engineer's watch.

"A sign of what?"

"That it's time."

Barthian waited.

"…time to build a Resistance."

There was a sudden banging on the newly repaired front door, and another familiar voice called out.

"Open up!" called Grimm. "I know you're in there."

"Oops," said the hooded man. "We delayed too long."

Barthian shook his head. "I did tell you!"

"Blaming people never got anyone anywhere," the hooded man said, taking off his cloak and dropping his mask. He wasn't an old man, perhaps ten or so years younger than Germain, but his bearded face and dark eyes carried more than the sum of his life's worth of experience.

Barthian immediately warmed to him, now that he could actually see him. "Have we met before?"

"Yes, I rescued you from the pirate ship not two days ago!"

"No, before that," Barthian said.

"I don't think so, no."

Grimm pounded on the door. When no one opened it, he ordered one of the automatons with him to break it down.

Something whirred, and an almighty crash sounded…but the door remained intact. Click-Clack had outdone himself with those repairs and metal reinforcements!

"What do you mean you can't get through it?" Grimm roared. "Well then saw through it!"

"Not again!" groaned Barthian.

"Easy for you to say…bzzt!" said Click-Clack.

"I need a better disguise," the formerly-hooded man said. "That black thing's getting old. Ooh, what's that?"

He rushed to the bed where the scarlet cloak was lying. He felt the cloth between his fingers like Barthian had, and saw the name EVERBRIGHT in gold stitching inside the hem.

"Well, I'll be," he said. "Do you mind?"

He pulled on the cloak, and it fit him perfectly. He pulled the mask back over his face, then replaced the goggles over his eyes. Finally, he pulled the hood over his head.

"Perfect!" he said. "What are you wearing?"

"What do you mean?" Barthian asked, as a motor revved and a saw began screeching against the door's reinforcements.

"Well, you're coming with me, aren't you?" The man gestured at Barthian's torn and stained clothes. "You can't be wearing those old things, not if we're going to shoot our way out! A break-out demands a little style."

Click-Clack squealed with delight.

Barthian stared, certain he must not have heard that right. "Sh… shoot our way out?"

"No other way to escape, I'm afraid." The hooded man shrugged.

"Where are we going?"

"Where would you like to go?"

Barthian didn't need time to come up with an answer—he knew right away. "I want to go and find my Mom and Dad."

"Your Mom and Dad?" The hooded man drew back in surprise. "You mean Magda and Jude Everbright?"

The sawing noises changed pitch as the metal bands across the door began giving way.

"Yes," said Barthian. "Is that a problem?"

"Not at all," the hooded man answered, with a chuckle. "I haven't seen them for years. It will be an interesting reunion."

The hooded man went to the door and cocked his pistols. "Well? Are you coming or not?" he asked. "The Fogworks is a good day's walk. Breaking in and rescuing your parents is going to take some planning."

Barthian looked around for clothing that was more fugitive. He found Germain's work belt, which he strapped around his waist, as well as an old hooded cloak and a scarf that he wrapped around his lower face.

"Much better," the Scarlet Man said, smiling. "Now—you ready?"

A board fell away from the door, and the sawing grew louder.

"Ready!" said Barthian, grinning at the hooded man. "You take the lead, and I'll follow!"

৯

THE END
of Book 1

CPSIA information can be obtained
at www.ICGtesting.com
Printed in the USA
LVHW090046260920
667015LV00017B/1718

9 780473 509286